THE MERRIE TALES OF JACQUES TOURNEBROCHE

THE MERRIE TALES OF JACQUES TOURNEBROCHE

AND CHILD LIFE IN TOWN AND COUNTRY

BY
ANATOLE FRANCE

A TRANSLATION BY
ALFRED ALLINSON

Short Story Index Reprint Series

 BOOKS FOR LIBRARIES PRESS
FREEPORT, NEW YORK

First Published 1909
Reprinted 1970

STANDARD BOOK NUMBER:
8369-3504-7

LIBRARY OF CONGRESS CATALOG CARD NUMBER:
77-121548

PRINTED IN THE UNITED STATES OF AMERICA

CONTENTS

THE MERRIE TALES OF JACQUES TOURNEBROCHE

PAGE

OLIVIER'S BRAG	9
THE MIRACLE OF THE MAGPIE	27
BROTHER JOCONDE	55
FIVE FAIR LADIES OF PICARDY, OF POITOU, OF TOURAINE, OF LYONS, AND OF PARIS	83
A GOOD LESSON WELL LEARNT	91
SATAN'S TONGUE-PIE	105
CONCERNING AN HORRIBLE PICTURE	109
MADEMOISELLE DE DOUCINE'S NEW YEAR'S PRESENT	117
MADEMOISELLE ROXANE	129

CHILD LIFE IN TOWN AND COUNTRY

FANCHON	159
THE FANCY-DRESS BALL	172
THE SCHOOL	175
MARIE	179
THE PANDEAN PIPES	182
ROGER'S STUD	185
COURAGE	187

CONTENTS

	PAGE
CATHERINE'S "AT HOME"	190
LITTLE SEA-DOGS	193
GETTING WELL	196
ACROSS THE MEADOWS	199
THE MARCH PAST	208
DEAD LEAVES	211
SUZANNE	214
FISHING	217
THE PENALTIES OF GREATNESS	220
A CHILD'S DINNER PARTY	223
THE ARTIST	226
JACQUELINE AND MIRAUT	229

OLIVIER'S BRAG

OLIVIER'S BRAG

THE Emperor Charlemagne and his twelve peers, having taken the palmer's staff at Saint-Denis, made a pilgrimage to Jerusalem. They prostrated themselves before the tomb of Our Lord, and sat in the thirteen chairs of the great hall wherein Jesus Christ and his Apostles met together to celebrate the blessed sacrifice of the Mass. Then they fared to Constantinople, being fain to see King Hugo, who was renowned for his magnificence.

The King welcomed them in his Palace, where, beneath a golden dome, birds of ruby, wrought with a wondrous art, sat and sang in bushes of emerald.

He seated the Emperor of France and the twelve Counts about a table loaded with stags, boars, cranes, wild geese, and peacocks, served in pepper. And he offered his guests, in oxhorns, the wines of Greece and Asia to drink. Charlemagne and his companions quaffed all these wines in honour of the King and his daughter, the Princess Helen. After supper Hugo led them to the chamber where they were to sleep. Now this chamber was circular, and a column, springing in the midst thereof, carried the vaulted roof. Nothing could be finer to look upon. Against the walls, which were hung with gold and purple, twelve beds were ranged, while another greater than the rest stood beside the pillar.

Charlemagne lay in this, and the Counts stretched themselves round about him on the others. The wine they had drunk ran hot in their veins, and their brains were afire. They could not sleep, and fell to making brags instead, and laying of wagers, as is the way of the knights of France, each striving to outdo the other in warranting himself to do some doughty deed for to manifest his prowess. The Emperor opened the game. He said:

"Let them fetch me, a-horseback and fully armed, the best knight King Hugo hath. I

OLIVIER'S BRAG

will lift my sword and bring it down upon him in such wise it shall cleave helm and hauberk, saddle and steed, and the blade shall delve a foot deep underground."

Guillaume d'Orange spake up after the Emperor and made the second brag.

"I will take," said he, "a ball of iron sixty men can scarce lift, and hurl it so mightily against the Palace wall that it shall beat down sixty fathoms' length thereof."

Ogier, the Dane, spake next.

"Ye see yon proud pillar which bears up the vault. To-morrow will I tear it down and break it like a straw."

After which Renaud de Montauban cried with an oath:

"'Od's life! Count Ogier, whiles you overset the pillar, I will clap the dome on my shoulders and hale it down to the seashore."

Gérard de Rousillon it was made the fifth brag.

He boasted he would uproot single-handed, in one hour, all the trees in the Royal pleasaunce.

Aïmer took up his parable when Gérard was done.

"I have a magic hat," said he, "made of a sea-calf's skin, which renders me invisible. I will set it on my head, and to-morrow, whenas King Hugo is seated at meat, I will eat up his fish and drink down his wine, I will tweak his nose and buffet his ears. Not knowing whom or what to blame, he will clap all his serving-men in gaol and scourge them sore,—and we shall laugh."

"For me," declared Huon de Bordeaux, whose turn it was, "for me, I am so nimble I will trip up to the King and cut off his beard and eyebrows without his knowing aught about the matter. 'T is a piece of sport I will show you to-morrow. And I shall have no need of a sea-calf hat either!"

Doolin de Mayence made his brag too. He promised to eat up in one hour all the figs and all the oranges and all the lemons in the King's orchards.

Next the Duc Naisme said in this wise:

"By my faith! *I* will go into the banquet hall, I will catch up flagons and cups of gold and fling them so high they will never light down again save to tumble into the moon."

OLIVIER'S BRAG

Bernard de Brabant then lifted his great voice:

"I will do better yet," he roared. "Ye know the river that flows by Constantinople is broad and deep, for it is come nigh its mouth by then, after traversing Egypt, Babylon, and the Earthly Paradise. Well, I will turn it from its bed and make it flood the Great Square of the City."

Gérard de Viane said:

"Put a dozen knights in line of array. And I will tumble all the twelve on their noses, only by the wind of my sword."

It was the Count Roland laid the twelfth wager, in the fashion following:

"I will take my horn, I will go forth of the city and I will blow such a blast all the gates of the town will drop from their hinges."

Olivier alone had said no word yet. He was young and courteous, and the Emperor loved him dearly.

"Olivier, my son," he asked, "will you not make your brag like the rest of us?"

"Right willingly, sire," Olivier replied.

"Do you know the name of Hercules of Greece?"

"Yea, I have heard some discourse of him," said Charlemagne. "He was an idol of the misbelievers, like the false god Mahound."

"Not so, sire," said Olivier. "Hercules of Greece was a knight among the Pagans and King of a Pagan kingdom. He was a gallant champion and stoutly framed in all his limbs. Visiting the Court of a certain Emperor who had fifty daughters, virgins, he wedded them all on one and the same night, and that so well and throughly that next morning they all avowed themselves well-contented women and with naught left to learn. He had not slighted ever a one of them. Well, sire, an you will, I will lay my wager to do after the fashion of Hercules of Greece."

"Nay, beware, Olivier, my son," cried the Emperor, "beware what you do; the thing would be a sin. I felt sure this King Hercules was a Saracen!"

"Sire," returned Olivier, "know this — I warrant me to show in the same space of time the selfsame prowess with one virgin that Hercules of Greece did with fifty. And the maid shall be none other but the Princess Helen, King Hugo's daughter."

"Good and well," agreed Charlemagne; "that will be to deal honestly and as a good Christian should. But you were in the wrong, my son, to drag the fifty virgins of King Hercules into your business, wherein, the Devil fly away with me else, I can see but one to be concerned."

"Sire," answered Olivier mildly, "there is but one of a truth. But she shall win such satisfaction of me that, an I number the tokens of my love, you will to-morrow see fifty crosses scored on the wall, and that is *my* brag."

The Count Olivier was yet speaking when lo! the column which bare the vault opened. The pillar was hollow and contrived in such sort that a man could lie hid therein at his ease to see and hear everything. Charlemagne and the twelve Counts had never a notion of this; so they were sore surprised to behold the King of Constantinople step forth. He was white with anger and his eyes flashed fire.

He said in a terrible voice:

"So this is how ye show your gratitude for the hospitality I offer you. Ye are ill-mannered guests. For a whole hour have ye been insulting me with your bragging wagers. Well, know this,—you, Sir Emperor, and ye, his knights; if to-morrow ye do not all of you make good your boasts, I will have your heads cut off."

Having said his say, he stepped back within the pillar, which shut to again closely behind him. For a while the twelve paladins were dumb with wonder and consternation. The Emperor was the first to break the silence.

"Comrades," he said, "'t is true we have bragged too freely. Mayhap we have spoken things better unsaid. We have drunk overmuch wine, and have shown unwisdom. The chiefest fault is mine; I am your Emperor, and I gave you the bad example. I will devise with you to-morrow of the means whereby we may save us from this perilous pass; meantime, it behoves us to get to sleep. I wish you a good night. God have you in his keeping!"

A moment later the Emperor and the twelve

peers were snoring under their coverlets of silk and cloth of gold.

They awoke on the morrow, their minds still distraught and deeming the thing was but a nightmare. But anon soldiers came to lead them to the Palace, that they might make good their brags before the King's face.

"Come," cried the Emperor, "come; and let us pray God and His Holy Mother. By Our Lady's help shall we easily make good our brags."

He marched in front with a more than human majesty of port. Arriving anon at the King's Palace, Charlemagne, Naisme, Aimer, Huon, Doolin, Guillaume, Ogier, Bernard, Renaud, the two Gérards, and Roland fell on their knees and, joining their hands in prayer, made this supplication to the Holy Virgin:

"Lady, which art in Paradise, look on us now in our extremity; for love of the Realm of the Lilies, which is thine own, protect the Emperor of France and his twelve peers, and give them the puissance to make good their brags."

Thereafter they rose up comforted and fulfilled of bright courage and gallant confidence, for they knew that Our Lady would answer their prayer.

King Hugo, seated on a golden throne, accosted them, saying:

"The hour is come to make good your brags. But an if ye fail so to do, I will have your heads cut off. Begone therefore, straightway, escorted by my men-at-arms, each one of you to the place meet for the doing of the fine things ye have insolently boasted ye will accomplish."

At this order they separated and went divers ways, each followed by a little troop of armed men. Whiles some returned to the hall where they had passed the night, others betook them to the gardens and orchards. Bernard de Brabant made for the river, Roland hied him to the ramparts, and all marched valiantly. Only Olivier and Charlemagne tarried in the Palace, waiting, the one for the knight that he had sworn to cleave in twain, the other for the maiden he was to wed.

But in very brief while a fearful sound arose,

awful as the last trump that shall proclaim to mankind the end of the world. It reached the Great Hall of the Palace, set the birds of ruby trembling on their emerald perches and shook King Hugo on his throne of gold.

'Twas a noise of walls crumbling into ruin and floods roaring, and high above the din blared out an ear-splitting trumpet blast. Meanwhile messengers had come hurrying in from all quarters of the city, and thrown themselves trembling at the King's feet, bearing strange and terrible tidings.

"Sire," said one, "sixty fathoms' length of the city walls is fallen in at one crash."

"Sire," cried another, "the pillar which bare up your vaulted hall is broken down, and the dome thereof we have seen walking like a tortoise toward the sea."

"Sire," faltered a third, "the river, with its ships and its fishes, is pouring through the streets, and will soon be beating against your Palace walls."

King Hugo, white with terror, muttered:

"By my faith! these men are wizards."

"Well, Sir King," Charlemagne addressed

him with a smile on his lips, "the Knight I wait for is long of coming."

The King sent for him, and he came. He was a knight of stately stature and well armed. The good Emperor clave him in twain, as he had said.

Now while these things were a-doing, Olivier thought to himself:

"The intervention of Our Most Blessed Lady is plain to see in these marvels; and I am rejoiced to behold the manifest tokens she vouchsafes of her love for the Realm of France. Not in vain have the Emperor and his companions implored the succour of the Holy Virgin, Mother of God. Alas! *I* shall pay for all the rest, and have my head cut off. For I cannot well ask the Virgin Mary to help me make good *my* brag. 'Tis an enterprise of a sort wherein 'twould be indiscreet to crave the interference of Her who is the *Lily of Purity*, the *Tower of Ivory*, the *Guarded Door* and the *Fenced Orchard-Close*. And, lacking aid from on high, I am sore afraid I may not do so much as I have said."

Thus ran Olivier's thoughts, when King Hugo roughly accosted him with the words:

"'T is now your turn, Count, to fulfil your promise."

"Sire," replied Olivier, "I am waiting with great impatience for the Princess your daughter. For you must needs do me the priceless grace of giving me her hand."

"That is but fair," said King Hugo. "I will therefore bid her come to you and a chaplain with her for to celebrate the marriage."

At church, during the ceremony, Olivier reflected:

"The maid is sweet and comely as ever a man could desire, and too fain am I to clip her in my arms to regret the brag I have made."

That evening, after supper, the Princess Helen and the Count Olivier were escorted by twelve ladies and twelve knights to a chamber, wherein the twain were left alone together.

There they passed the night, and on the morrow guards came and led them both before King Hugo. He was on his throne, surrounded by his knights. Near by stood Charlemagne and the peers.

"Well, Count Olivier," demanded the King, "is your brag made good?"

Olivier held his peace, and already was King Hugo rejoiced at heart to think his new son-in-law's head must fall. For of all the brags and boasts, it was Olivier's had angered him worst.

"Answer," he stormed. "Do you dare to tell me your brag is accomplished?"

Thereupon the Princess Helen, blushing and smiling, spake with eyes downcast and in a faint voice, yet clear withal, and said, — "Yea!"

Right glad were Charlemagne and the peers to hear the Princess say this word.

"Well, well," said Hugo, "these Frenchmen have God and the Devil o' their side. It was fated I should cut off none of these knights' heads. . . . Come hither, son-in-law," — and he stretched forth his hand to Olivier, who kissed it.

The Emperor Charlemagne embraced the Princess and said to her:

OLIVIER'S BRAG

"Helen, I hold you for my daughter and my son's wife. You will go along with us to France, and you will live at our Court."

Then, as his lips lay on the Princess's cheek, he rounded softly in her ear:

"You spake as a loving-hearted woman should. But tell me this in closest confidence,—Did you speak the truth?"

She answered:

"Sire, Olivier is a gallant man and a courteous. He was so full of pretty ways and dainty devices for to distract my mind, *I* never thought of counting. Nor yet did *he* keep score. Needs therefore must I hold him quit of his promise."

King Hugo made great rejoicings for his daughter's nuptials. Thereafter Charlemagne and his twelve peers returned back to France, taking with them the Princess Helen.

THE MIRACLE OF THE MAGPIE

THE MIRACLE OF THE MAGPIE

I

LENT, of the year 1429, presented a strange marvel of the Calendar, a conjunction that moved the admiration not only of the common crowd of the Faithful, but eke of Clerks, well learned in Arithmetic. For Astronomy, mother of the Calendar, was Christian in those days. In 1429 Good Friday fell on the Feast of the Annunciation, so that one and the same day combined the commemoration of the two several mysteries which did commence and consummate the redemption of mankind, and in wondrous wise superimposed one on top of the other, Jesus conceived in the Virgin's womb and Jesus dying on the Cross. This Friday, whereon the mystery of joy came so to coincide exactly with the mystery of sorrow, was named the "Grand Friday," and was kept holy with solemn Feasts on Mount Anis, in the Church of the Annunciation. For many years, by gift of the Popes of Rome, the sanctuary of Mount Anis had possessed the privilege of the plenary indulgences of a great jubilee, and the late-deceased Bishop of Le Puy, Élie de Lestrange, had gotten Pope Martin to restore this *pardon*. It was a favour of the sort the Popes scarce ever refused, when asked in due and proper form.

The *pardon* of the Grand Friday drew a great crowd of pilgrims and traders to Le Puy-en-Velay. As early as mid February folk from distant lands set out thither in cold and wind and rain. For the most part they fared on foot, staff in hand. Whenever they could, these pilgrims travelled in companies, to the end they might not be robbed and held to ransom by the armed bands that infested the country parts, and by the barons who exacted toll on the confines of their lands. Inasmuch as the mountain districts were especially dangerous, they tarried in the neighbouring towns, Clermont, Issoire, Brioude, Lyons, Issingeaux, Alais, till they were gathered in a great host, and then went forth on their road in the snow. During Holy Week a strange multitude thronged the hilly streets of Le Puy,—pedlars from Languedoc and Provence and Catalonia, leading their mules laded with leather goods, oil, wool, webs of cloth, or wines of Spain in goat-skins; lords a-horseback and ladies in wains, artisans and traders pacing on their mules, with wife or daughter perched behind. Then came the poor pilgrim folk, limping along, halting and hobbling, stick in hand and bag on back, panting up the stiff climb. Last were the flocks of oxen and sheep being driven to the slaughter-houses.

Now, leant against the wall of the Bishop's palace, stood Florent Guillaume, looking as long and dry and black as an espalier vine in winter, and devoured pilgrims and cattle with his eyes.

"Look," he called to Marguerite the lace-maker, "look at yonder fine heads of bestial."

And Marguerite, squatted beside her bobbins, called back:

"Yea, fine beasts, and fat withal!"

Both the twain were very bare and scant of the goods of this world, and even then were feeling bitterly the pinch of hunger. And folk said it came of their own fault. At that very moment Pierre Grandmange the tripe-seller was saying as much, where he stood in his tripe-shop, pointing a finger at them. "'T would be sinful," he was crying, "to give an alms to such good-for-nothing varlets." The tripe-seller would fain have been very charitable, but he feared to lose his soul by giving to evil-livers, and all the fat citizens of Le Puy had the selfsame scruples.

To say truth, we must needs allow that, in the heyday of her hot youth, Marguerite the lace-maker had not matched St. Lucy in purity, St. Agatha in constancy, and St. Catherine in staidness. As for Florent Guillaume, he had been the best scrivener in the city. For years he had not had his equal for engrossing the Hours of Our Lady of Le Puy. But he had been over fond of merrymakings and

THE MIRACLE OF THE MAGPIE

junketings. Now his hand had lost its cunning, and his eye its clearness; he could no more trace the letters on the parchment with the needful steadiness of touch. Even so, he might have won his livelihood by teaching apprentices in his shop at the sign of the Image of Our Lady, under the choir buttresses of *The Annunciation*, for he was a fellow of good counsel and experience. But having had the ill fortune to borrow of Maître Jacquet Coquedouille the sum of six livres ten sous, and having paid him back at divers terms eighty livres two sous, he had found himself at the last to owe yet six livres two sous to the account of his creditor, which account was approved correct by the judges, for Jacquet Coquedouille was a sound arithmetician. This was the reason why the scrivenry of Florent Guillaume, under the choir buttresses of *The Annunciation*, was sold, on Saturday the fifth day of March, being the Feast of St. Theophilus, to the profit of Maître Jacquet Coquedouille. Since that time the poor penman had never a place to call his own. But by the good help of Jean Magne the bell-ringer and with the protection of Our Lady, whose Hours he had aforetime written, Florent Guillaume found a perch o' nights in the steeple of the Cathedral.

The scrivener and the lace-maker had much ado to live. Marguerite only kept body and soul together by chance and charity, for she had long lost her good looks and she hated the lace-making. They helped each other. Folks said so by way of reproach; they had been better advised to account it to them for righteousness. Florent Guillaume was a learned clerk. Well knowing every word of the history of the beautiful Black Virgin of Le Puy and the ordering of the ceremonies of the great *pardon*, he had conceived the notion he might serve as guide to the pilgrims, deeming he would surely light on someone compassionate enough to pay him a supper in guerdon of his fine stories. But the first folk he had offered his services to had bidden him begone because his ragged coat bespoke neither good guidance nor clerkly wit; so he had come back, downhearted and crestfallen, to the Bishop's wall, where he had his bit of sunshine and

THE MIRACLE OF THE MAGPIE

his kind gossip Marguerite. "They reckon," he said bitterly, "I am not learned enough to number them the relics and recount the miracles of Our Lady. Do they think my wits have escaped away through the holes in my gaberdine?"

"'T is not the wits," replied Marguerite, "escape by the holes in a body's clothes, but the good natural heat. I am sore a-cold. And it is but too true that, man and woman, they judge us by our dress. The gallants would find me comely enough yet if I was accoutred like my Lady the Comtesse de Clermont."

Meanwhile, all the length of the street in front of them the pilgrims were elbowing and fighting their way to the Sanctuary, where they were to win pardon for their sins.

"They will surely suffocate anon," said Marguerite. "Twenty-two years agone, on the Grand Friday, two hundred persons died stifled under the porch of *The Annunciation*. God have their souls in keeping! Ay, those were the good times, when I was young!"

"'T is very true indeed, that year you tell of, two hundred pilgrims crushed each other to death and departed from this world to the other. And next day was never a sign to be seen of aught untoward."

As he so spake, Florent Guillaume noted a pilgrim, a very fat man, who was not hurrying to get him assoiled with the same hot haste as the rest, but kept rolling his wide eyes to right and left with a look of distress and fear. Florent Guillaume stepped up to him and louted low.

"Messire," he accosted him, "one may see at a glance you are a sensible man and an experienced; you do not rush blindly to the *pardon* like a sheep to the slaughter. The rest of the folk go helter-skelter thither, the nose of one under the tail of the other; but you follow a wiser fashion. Grant me the boon to be your guide, and you will not repent your bargain."

The pilgrim, who proved to be a gentleman of Limoges, answered in the patois of his countryside, that he had no use for a scurvy beggarman and could very well find his own way to *The Annunciation* for to receive pardon for his faults. And therewith he set his face

THE MIRACLE OF THE MAGPIE

resolutely to the hill. But Florent Guillaume cast himself at his feet, and tearing at his hair:

"Stop! stop! messire," he cried; "i' God's name and by all the Saints, I warn you go no farther! 'T will be your death, and you are not the man we could see perish without grief and dolour. A few steps more and you are a dead man! They are suffocating up yonder. Already full six hundred pilgrims have given up the ghost. And this is but a small beginning! Do you not know, messire, that twenty-two years agone, in the year of grace one thousand four hundred and seven, on the selfsame day and at the selfsame hour, under yonder porch, nine thousand six hundred and thirty-eight persons, without reckoning women and children, trampled each other underfoot and perished miserably? An you met the same fate, I should never smile again. To see you is to love you, messire; to know you is to conceive a sudden and overmastering desire to serve you."

The Limousin gentleman had halted in no small surprise and turned pale to hear such discourse and see the fellow tearing out his hair in fistfuls. In his terror he was for turning back the way he had come. But Florent Guillaume, on his knees in the mud, held him back by the skirt of his jacket.

"Never go that way, messire! not that way. You might meet Jacquet Coquedouille, and you would be all in an instant turned into stone. Better encounter the basilisk than Jacquet Coquedouille. I will tell you what you must do if, like the wise and prudent man your face proclaims you to be, you would live long and make your peace with God. Hearken to me; I am a scholar, a Bachelor. To-day the holy relics will be borne through the streets and crossways of the city. You will find great solace in touching the carven shrines which enclose the cornelian cup wherefrom the child Jesus drank, one of the wine-jars of the Marriage at Cana, the cloth of the Last Supper, and the holy foreskin. If you take my advice, we will go wait for them, under cover, at a cookshop I wot of, before which they will pass without fail."

Then, in a wheedling voice, without loosing his hold of the pilgrim's jacket, he pointed to the lace-maker and said:

THE MIRACLE OF THE MAGPIE

"Messire, you must give six sous to yonder worthy woman, that she may go buy us wine, for she knows where good liquor is to be gotten."

The Limousin gentleman, who was a simple soul after all, went where he was led, and Florent Guillaume supped on the leg and wing of a goose, the bones whereof he put in his pocket as a present for Madame Ysabeau, his fellow lodger in the timbers of the steeple, — to wit, Jean Magne the bell-ringer's magpie.

He found her that night perched on the beam where she was used to roost, beside the hole in the wall which was her storeroom wherein she hoarded walnuts and hazel-nuts, almonds and beech-nuts. She had awoke at the noise of his coming and flapped her wings; so he greeted her very courteously, addressing her in these obliging terms:

"Magpie most pious, lady recluse, bird of the cloister, Margot of the Nunnery, sable-frocked Abbess, Church fowl of the lustrous coat, all hail!"

Then offering her the goose bones nicely folded in a cabbage leaf:

"Lady," he said, "I bring you here the scraps remaining of a good dinner a gentleman from Limoges gave me. His countrymen are radish eaters; but I have taught this one to prefer an Anis goose to all the radishes in the Limousin."

Next day and the rest of the week Florent Guillaume, — for he could never light on his fat friend again nor yet any other good pilgrim with a well-lined travelling wallet, — fasted *a solis ortu usque ad occasum*, from rising sun to dewy eve. Marguerite the lace-maker did likewise. This was very meet and right, seeing the time was Holy Week.

II

NOW on Holy Easter Day, Maître Jacquet Coquedouille, a notable citizen of the place, was peeping through a hole in a shutter of his house and watching the countless throng of pilgrims passing down the steep street. They were wending homewards, happy to have won their pardon; and the sight of them greatly magnified his veneration for the Black Virgin. For he deemed a lady so much sought after must needs be a puissant dame. He was old, and his only hope lay in God's mercy. Yet was he but ill-assured of his eternal salvation, for he remembered how many a time he had ruthlessly fleeced the widow and the orphan. Moreover, he had robbed Florent Guillaume of his scrivenry at the sign of Our Lady. He was used to lend at high interest on sound security. Yet could no man infer he was a usurer, forasmuch as he was a Christian, and it was only the Jews practised usury,—the Jews, and, if you will, the Lombards and the men of Cahors.

Now Jacquet Coquedouille went about the matter quite otherwise than the Jews. He never said, like Jacob, Ephraim, and Manasses, "I am lending you money." What he did say was, "I am putting money into your business to help your trafficking," a different thing altogether. For usury and lending upon interest were forbidden by the Church, but trafficking was lawful and permitted.

And yet at the thought how he had brought many Christian folk to poverty and despair, Jacquet Coquedouille felt the pangs of remorse, as he pictured the sword of Divine Justice hanging over his head. So on this holy Easter Day he was fain to secure him against the Last Judgment by winning the protection of Our Lady. He thought to himself she would plead for him at the judgment seat of her divine Son, if only he gave her a handsome fee. So he went to the great chest where he kept his gold, and, after mak-

THE MIRACLE OF THE MAGPIE

ing sure the chamber door was shut fast, he opened the chest, which was full of angels, florins, esterlings, nobles, gold crowns, gold ducats, and golden sous, and all the coins ever struck by Christian or Saracen. He extracted with a sigh of regret twelve deniers of fine gold and laid them on the table, which was crowded with balances, files, scissors, gold-scales, and account books. After shutting his chest again and triple-locking it, he numbered the deniers, renumbered them, gazed long at them with looks of affection, and addressed them in words so soft and sweet, so affable and ingratiating, so gentle and courteous, it seemed rather the music of the spheres than human speech.

"Oh, little angels!" sighed the good old man. "Oh, my dear little angels! Oh, my pretty gold sheep, with the fine, precious fleece!"

And taking the pieces between his fingers with as much reverence as it had been the body of Our Lord, he put them in the balance and made sure they were of the full weight, — or very near, albeit a trifle clipped already by the Lombards and the Jews, through whose hands they had passed. After which he spoke to them yet more graciously than before:

"Oh, my pretty sheep, my sweet, pretty lambs, there, let me shear you! 'T will do you no hurt at all."

Then, seizing his great scissors, he clipped off shreds of gold here and there, as he was used to clip every piece of money before parting with it. And he gathered the clippings carefully in a wooden bowl that was already half full of bits of gold. He was ready to give twelve angels to the Holy Virgin; but he felt no way bound to depart from his use and wont. This done, he went to the aumry where his pledges lay, and drew out a little blue purse, broidered with silver, which a dame of the petty trading sort had left with him in her distress. He remembered that blue and white are Our Lady's colours.

That day and the next he did nothing further. But in the night, betwixt Monday and Tuesday, he had cramps, and dreamt the devils were pulling him by the feet. This he took for a warning of God and our Blessed Lady, tarried within doors pondering the matter all the day, and then toward evening went to lay his offering at the feet of the Black Virgin.

III

THAT same day, as night was closing in, Florent Guillaume thought ruefully of returning to his airy bedchamber. He had fasted the livelong day, sore against the grain, holding that a good Christian ought not to fast in the glorious Resurrection week. Before mounting to his bed in the steeple, he went to offer a pious prayer to the Lady of Le Puy. She was still there in the midst of the Church at the spot where she had offered herself on the Grand Friday to the veneration of the Faithful. Small and black, crowned with jewels, in a mantle blazing with gold and precious stones and pearls, she held on her knees the Child Jesus, who was as black as his mother and passed his head through a slit in her cloak. It was the miraculous image which St. Louis had received as a

THE MIRACLE OF THE MAGPIE

gift from the Soldan of Egypt and had carried with his own hands to the Church of Anis.

All the pilgrims were gone now, and the Church was dark and empty. The last offerings of the Faithful were spread at the feet of the beautiful Black Virgin, displayed on a table lit with wax tapers. You could see amongst the rest a head, hearts, hands, feet, a woman's breasts of silver, a little boat of gold, eggs, loaves, Aurillac cheeses, and in a bowl full of deniers, sous, and groats, a little blue purse broidered with silver. Over against the table, in a huge chair, dozed the priest who guarded the offerings.

Florent Guillaume dropped on his knees before the holy image, and said over to himself this pious prayer:

"Lady, an it be true that the holy prophet Jeremias, having beheld thee with the eyes of faith ere ever thou wast conceived, carved with his hands out of cedar-wood in thy likeness the holy image before which I am at this present kneeling; an it be true that afterward King Ptolemy, instructed of the miracles wrought by this same holy image, took it from the Jewish priests, bare it to Egypt and set it up, covered with precious stones, in the temple of the idols; an it be true that Nebuchadnezzar, conqueror of the Egyptians, seized it in his turn and had it laid amongst his treasure, where the Saracens found it when they captured Babylon; an it be true that the Soldan loved it in his heart above all things, and was used to adore it at the least once every day; an it be true that the said Soldan had never given it to our saintly King Louis, but that his wife, who was a Saracen dame, yet prized chivalry and knightly prowess, resolved to make it a gift to the best knight and worthiest champion of all Christendom; in a word, an this image be miraculous, as I do firmly credit, have it do a miracle, Lady, in favour of the poor clerk who hath many a time writ thy praises on the vellum of the service books. He hath sanctified his sinful hands by engrossing in a fair writing, with great red capitals at the beginning of each clause, 'the fifteen joys of Our Lady,' in the vulgar tongue and in rhyme, for the comforting of the afflicted. 'T is pious work this. Think of

THE MIRACLE OF THE MAGPIE

it, Lady, and heed not his sins. Give him somewhat to eat. 'Twill both do me much profit, and bring thee great honour, for the miracle will appear no mean one to all them that know the world. Thou hast this day gotten gold, eggs, cheeses, and a little blue purse broidered with silver. Lady, I grudge thee none of the gifts that have been made thee. Thou dost well deserve them, yea, and more than they. I do not so much as ask thee to make them give me back what a thief hath robbed me of, a thief by name Jacquet Coquedouille, one of the most honoured citizens of this thy town of Le Puy. No, all I ask of thee is not to let me die of hunger. And if thou grant me this boon, I will indite a full and fair history of thine holy image here present."

So prayed Florent Guillaume. The soft murmur of his petition was answered only by the deep-chested, placid snore of the sleeping priest. The poor scrivener rose from his knees, stepped noiselessly adown the nave, for he was grown so light his footfall could scarce be heard, and, fasting as he was, climbed the tower stairs that had as many steps as there are days in the year.

Meanwhile Madame Ysabeau, slipping under the cloister gate, entered her Church. The pilgrims had driven her away, for she loved peace and solitude. The bird came forward cautiously, putting one foot slowly in front of the other, then stopped and craned her neck, casting a suspicious look to right and left. Then giving a graceful little jump and shaking out her tail feathers, she hopped up to the Black Madonna. Then she stood stock still a few moments, scrutinising the sleeping watchman and questioning the darkness and silence with eyes and ears alert. At last with a mighty flutter of wings she alighted on the table of offerings.

IV

EANWHILE Florent Guillaume had settled himself for the night in the steeple. It was bitter cold. The wind came blowing in through the luffer-boards and fluted and organed among the bells to rejoice the heart of the cats and owls. And this was not the only objection to the lodging. Since the earthquake of 1427, which had shaken the whole church, the spire was dropping to pieces stone by stone and threatened to collapse altogether in the first storm. Our Lady suffered this dilapidation because of the people's sins.

Presently Florent Guillaume fell asleep, which is a token of his innocency of heart. What dreams he dreamt is clean forgot, except that he had a vision in his sleep of a lady of consummate beauty who came and kissed him on the mouth. But when his lips opened to return her salute, he swallowed two or three woodlice that were walking over his face and by their tickling had deluded his sleeping senses into the agreeable fancy. He awoke, and hearing a noise of wings beating above his head, he thought it was a devil, as was very natural for him to opine, seeing how the evil spirits flock in countless swarms to torment mankind, and above all at night time. But the moon just then breaking through the clouds, he recognised Madame Ysabeau and saw she was busy with her beak pushing into a crack in the wall that served her for storehouse a blue purse broidered with silver. He let her do as she list; but when she had left her hoard, he clambered onto a beam, took the purse, opened it, and saw it contained twelve good gold deniers, which he clapped in his belt, giving thanks to the incomparable Black Virgin of Le Puy. For he was a clerk and versed in the Scriptures, and he remembered how the Lord fed his prophet Elias by a raven; whence he inferred that the Holy Mother of God had sent by a magpie twelve deniers to her poor penman, Florent Guillaume.

On the morrow Florent and Marguerite the lace-maker ate a dish of tripe,—a treat they had craved for many a long year.

So ends the Miracle of the Magpie. May he who tells the tale live, as he would fain live, in good and gentle peace, and all good hap befall such folk as shall read the same.

BROTHER JOCONDE

BROTHER JOCONDE

THE Parisians were far from loving the English and found it hard to put up with them. When, after the obsequies of the late King Charles VI, the Duke of Bedford had the sword of the King of France borne before him, the people murmured. But what cannot be cured must be endured. Besides, though the capital hated the English, it loved the Burgundians. What more natural for citizen folk, and especially for money-changers and traders, than to admire Duke Philip, a prince of seemly presence and the richest nobleman in Christendom. As for the "little King of Bourges," a sorry-looking mortal and very poor, strongly suspected, moreover, of foul murder at the Bridge of Montereau, what had he about him to please folk withal? Scorn was the sentiment felt for him, and horror and loathing for his partisans. For ten years now had these been riding and raiding around the walls, pillaging and holding to ransom. No doubt the English and Burgundians did much the same; when, in the month of August, 1423, Duke Philip came to Paris, his men-at-arms had ravaged all the country about. And they were friends and allies of course; but after all they only came and went. The Armagnacs, on the contrary, were always in the field, stealing whatever they could lay their hands upon, firing farmsteads and churches, killing women and children, deflowering virgins and nuns, hanging men by the thumbs. In 1420 they threw themselves like devils let loose on the village of Champigny and burnt up altogether oats, wheat, lambs, cows, oxen, children, and women. They did the like and worse at Croissy. A very great clerk of the University declared they wrought all wickedness that can be wrought and conceived, and that more Christian folk had been martyred at their hands than ever Maximian or Diocletian did to death.

At the news that these accursed Armagnacs

were at the gates of Compiègne and occupying the neighbouring castles and their lands, the folk of Paris were sore afraid. They believed that the Dauphin's soldiers had sworn, if they entered Paris, to slay whomsoever they found there. They affirmed openly that Messire Charles de Valois had given up to his men's mercy town and townsmen, great and small, of every rank and condition, men and women, and that he proposed to drive the plough over the site of the city. The inhabitants mostly believed the tale; so they set the St. Andrew's cross on their coats, in token that they were of the party of the Burgundians. Their hatred was doubled, and their fears with it, when they learned that Brother Richard and the Maid Jeanne were at the head of King Charles' army. They knew nothing of the Maid save from the rumour of the victories she was reported to have won at Orleans. But they deemed she had vanquished the English by the Devil's aid, by means of spells and enchantments. The Masters of the University all said: "A creature in shape of a woman is with the Armagnacs. What it is, God knows!"

For Brother Richard, they knew him well. He had come to Paris before, and they had hearkened reverently to his sermons. He had even persuaded them to renounce those games of chance for which they had been used to forget meat and drink and the services of the Church. Now, at the tidings that Brother Richard was on foray with the Armagnacs and winning over for them by his well-hung tongue good towns like Troyes in Champagne, they called down on him the curse of God and his Saints. They tore out of their hats the leaden medals inscribed with the holy name of Jesus, which the good Brother had given them, and to show in what detestation they held him, resumed dice, bowls, draughts, and all other games they had renounced at his exhortation.

The city was strongly fortified, for in the days when King Jean was a prisoner of the English, the citizens of Paris, seeing the enemy in the heart of the Kingdom, had feared a siege and had hastened to put the walls in a state of defence. They had surrounded the place with moats and counter-moats. The moats, on the left bank of the river, were dug at the foot of the walls forming the old circle of fortification. But on the right bank there were faubourgs, both extensive and well built, outside the walls and almost touching them. The new moats enclosed a part of these, and the Dauphin Charles, King Jean's son, afterward had a wall built along the line of them. Nevertheless there was some feeling of insecurity, for the Cathedral Chapter took measures to put the relics and treasure out of reach of the enemy.

Meantime, on Sunday, August 21st, a Cordelier, by name Brother Joconde, entered the town. He had made pilgrimage to Jerusalem, and was said, like Brother Vincent Ferrier and Brother Bernardino of Sienna, to have enjoyed by the abounding grace of God many revelations anent the forthcoming end of the world. He gave out that he would preach his first sermon to the Parisians on Tuesday following, St. Bartholomew's day, in the Cloister of "The Innocents." On the eve of that day more than six thousand persons spent the night in the Cloister. At the foot of the platform wherefrom he was to preach, the women sat squatted on their heels, and amongst them Guillaumette Dyonis, who was blind from birth.

She was the child of an artisan who had been killed by the Burgundians in the woods of Boulogne-la-Grande. Her mother had been carried off by a Burgundian man-at-arms, and none knew what had become of her. Guillaumette was fifteen or sixteen years of age. She lived at "The Innocents" on what she made by spinning wool, at which trade there was not a better worker to be found in all the town. She went and came in the streets without the help of any and knew everything as well as those who can see. As she lived a good and holy life and fasted often, she was favoured with visions. In especial she had been accorded notable revelations by the Apostle St. John concerning the troubles that then beset the Kingdom of France. Now, as she was reciting her Hours at the foot of the platform, under the great Dance of Death, a woman called Simone la Bardine, who was seated on the ground beside her, asked her if the good Brother was not coming soon.

Guillaumette Dyonis could not see the tailed gown of green and the horned wimple which Simone la Bardine wore; yet she knew by instinct the woman was no honest dame. She felt a natural aversion for light women and the sort the soldiers called their sweethearts or "doxies," but it had been revealed to her that we should hold such in great pity and deal compassionately with them. Wherefore she answered Simone la Bardine gently:

"The good Father will come soon, please God. And we shall have no reason to regret having waited, for he is eloquent in prayer and his sermons turn the folk to devotion more even than those of Brother Richard, who spake in these Cloisters in the springtime. He knows more than any man living of the times that shall come and shall show us strange portents. I trow we shall gain great profit of his words."

"God grant it," sighed Simone la Bardine. "But are you not very sorry to be blind?"

"No. I wait to see God."

Simone la Bardine made her mantle into a cushion, and said:

"Life is all ups and downs. I live at the top of the Rue Saint-Antoine. 'T is the finest part of the city and the merriest, for the best hostelries are in the Place Baudet and thereabout. Before the Wars there was aye abundance there of hot cakes and fresh herrings and Auxerre wine by the tun. With the English famine entered the town. Now is there neither bread in the bin nor firewood on the hearth. One after other the Armagnacs and the Burgundians have drunk up all the wine, and there is naught left in the cellar but a little thin, sour cider and sloe-juice. Knights armed for the tourney, pilgrims with their cockle-shells and staves, traders with their chests full of knives and little service-books, where are they gone? They never come now to seek a lodging and good living in the Rue Saint-Antoine. But the wolves quit covert in the forests and prowl of nights in the faubourgs and devour little children."

"Put your trust in God," Guillaumette Dyonis answered her.

"Amen!" returned Simone la Bardine. "But I have not told you the worst. On the Thursday before St. John's day, at three after midnight, two Englishmen came knocking at my door. Not knowing but they had come to rob me or break up my chests and coffers out of mischief, or do some other devilment, I shouted to them from my window to go their ways, that I did not know them and I was not going to open the door. But they only hammered louder, swearing they were going to break in the door and come in and cut off my nose and ears. To stop their uproar I emptied a crockful of water on their heads; but the crock slipped out of my hands and broke on the back of one fellow's neck so unchancily that it felled him. His comrade called up the watch. I was haled to the Châtelet and clapped in prison, where I was very hardly handled, and only escaped by paying a heavy sum of money. I found my house pillaged from cellar to attic. From that day my affairs have gone from bad to worse, and I have naught in the wide world but the clothes I stand up in. In very despair I have come hither to hear the good Father, who they say abounds in comforting words."

"God, who loves you," said Guillaumette Dyonis, "has moved you in all this."

Then a great silence fell on the crowd as Brother Joconde appeared. His eyes flashed like lightning. When he opened his lips, his voice pealed out like thunder.

"I have come from Jerusalem," he began; "and to prove it, see in this wallet are roses of Jericho, a branch of the olive under which Our Saviour sweated drops of blood, and a handful of the earth of Calvary."

He gave a long narrative of his pilgrimage. And he added:

"In Syria I met Jews travelling in companies; I asked them whither they were bound, and they told me: 'We are flocking in crowds to Babylon, because in very deed the Messiah is born among men, and will restore us our heritage, and stablish us again in the Land of Promise.' So said these Jews of Syria. Now the Scriptures teach us that he they call the Messiah is, in truth, Antichrist, of whom it is said he must be born at Babylon, chief city of the kingdom of Persia, be reared at Bethsaïda, and dwell in his youth at Chorazin. That is

BROTHER JOCONDE

why Our Lord said: 'Woe unto thee, Chorazin! Woe unto thee, Bethsaïda!'

"The year that is at hand," went on Brother Joconde, "will bring the greatest marvels that have ever been beheld.

"The times are at hand. He is born, the man of sin, the son of perdition, the wicked man, the beast from out the abyss, the abomination of desolation. He comes from the tribe of Dan, of which it is written: 'Dan shall be a serpent in the way, an adder in the path.'

"Brethren, soon shall ye see returning to this earth the Prophets Elias and Enoch, Moses, Jeremias, and St. John Evangelist. And lo! the day of wrath is dawning, the day which 'solvet sæclum in favilla, teste David et Sibylla.' Wherefore now is the time to repent and do penance and renounce the false delights of this world."

At the good Brother's word bosoms heaved with remorse and deep-drawn sighs were heard. Not a few, both men and women, were near fainting when the preacher cried:

"I read in your souls that ye keep mandrakes at home, which will bring you to hell fire."

It was true. Many Parisians paid heavily to the old witch-wives, who profess unholy knowledge, for to buy mandrakes, and were used to keep them treasured in a chest. These magic roots have the likeness of a little man, hideously ugly and misshapen in a weird and diabolic fashion. They would dress them out magnificently, in fine linen and silks, and the mannikins brought them riches, chief source of all the ills of this world.

Next Brother Joconde thundered against women's extravagant attire.

"Leave off," he bade them, "your horns and your tails! Are ye not shamed so to bedizen yourselves like she-devils? Light bonfires, I say, in the public streets, and cast therein and burn your damnable head-gear, — pads and rolls, erections of leather and whalebone, wherewith ye stiffen out the front of your hoods."

He ended by exhorting them with so much zeal and loving-kindness not to lose their souls, but put themselves in the grace of God, that all who heard him wept hot tears. And Simone la Bardine wept more abundantly than any.

When, finally, coming down from his platform, Brother Joconde crossed the cloister and graveyard, the people fell on their knees as he went by. The women gave him their little ones to bless, or besought him to touch medals and rosaries for them. Some plucked threads from his gown, thinking to get healing by putting them, like relics of the Saints, on the places where they were afflicted. Guillaumette Dyonis followed the good Father as easily as if she saw him with her bodily eyes. Simone la Bardine trailed behind her, sobbing. She had pulled off her horned wimple and tied a kerchief round her head.

Thus they marched, the three of them, along the streets, where men and women, who had been at the preaching, were kindling fires before their doors to cast therein head-gear and mandrake roots. But on reaching the river bank, Brother Joconde sat down under an elm, and Guillaumette Dyonis came up to him and said:

"Father, it hath been revealed to me in vision that you are come to this Kingdom to restore the same to good peace and concord. I have had myself many revelations concerning the peace of the Kingdom."

Next Simone la Bardine took up her parable and said:

"Brother Joconde, I lived once in a fine house in the Rue Saint-Antoine, near by the Place Baudet, which is the fairest quarter of Paris, and the wealthiest. I had a matted chamber, mantles of cloth of gold, and gowns trimmed with miniver, enough to fill three great chests; I had a feather-bed, a dresser loaded with pewter, and a little book wherein you saw in pictures the story of Our Lord. But since the wars and pillagings that devastate the Kingdom, I have lost everything. The gallants never come now to take their pleasure in the Place Baudet. But the wolves come there instead to devour little children. The Burgundians and the English are as bad as the Armagnacs. Would you have me go with you?"

The Monk gazed a while in silence at the two women; and deeming it was Jesus Christ himself had led them to him, he received them for his Penitents, and thereafter the twain followed him wherever he went. Every day he preached to the people, now at "The Innocents," now at the Porte Saint-Honoré, or at the Halles. But he never went outside the Walls, by reason of the Armagnacs, who were raiding all the countryside round the city.

His words led many souls to a better life; and at the fourth sermon he preached in Paris, he received for Penitents Jeannette Chastenier, wife of a merchant-draper on the Pont-au-Change, and another woman, by name Opportune Jadoin, who nursed the sick at the Hôtel-Dieu and was no longer very young. He admitted likewise into his company a gardener of the Ville-l'Evêque, a lad of about sixteen, Robin by name, who bare on his feet and hands the stigmata of the crucifixion, and was shaken by a sore trembling of all his limbs. He often saw the Holy Virgin in corporeal presence, and heard her speech and savoured the divine odours of her glorified body. She had entrusted him with a message for the Regent of England and for the Duke of Burgundy. Meantime the army of Messire Charles of Valois entered the town of Saint-Denis. And no man durst from that day go out of Paris to harvest the fields or gather aught from the market-gardens which covered the plain to the northward of the city. Instantly famine prices ruled, and the inhabitants began to suffer cruelly. And they were further exasperated because they believed themselves betrayed. It was openly said that certain folk, and in especial certain men of Religion, suborned by Messire Charles of Valois, were watching for the best time to stir up trouble and bring in the enemy in an hour of panic and confusion. Haunted by this fear, which was not perhaps altogether baseless, the citizens who kept guard of the ramparts showed scant mercy to any men of evil looks whom they found loitering near the Gates and whom they might suspect, on the most trivial evidence, of making signals to the Armagnacs.

On Thursday, September 8th, the good

BROTHER JOCONDE

people of Paris awoke without any fear of being attacked before the next day. This day, September 8th, was the Feast of the Nativity of the Virgin, and it was an established custom with the two factions that tore the Kingdom in twain to keep holy the feast-days of Our Lord and His Blessed Mother.

Yet at this holy season the Parisians, on coming forth from Mass, learnt that, notwithstanding the sacredness of the day, the Armagnacs had appeared before the Porte Saint-Honoré and had set fire to the outwork which defended its approach. It was further reported that Messire Charles of Valois was posted, for the time being, along with Brother Richard and the Maid Jeanne, in the Hog Market without the Walls. The same afternoon, through all the city, on either side the bridges, shouts of fear arose—"Save yourselves! fly, the enemy are come in, all is lost!" The cries were heard even inside the Churches, where pious folks were singing Vespers. These came flying out in terror and ran to their houses to take refuge behind barred doors.

Now the men who went about raising these

cries were emissaries of Messire Charles of Valois. In fact, at that very time, the Company of the Maréchal de Rais was making assault on the Walls near by the Porte Saint-Honoré. The Armagnacs had brought up in carts great bundles of faggots and wattled hurdles to fill up the moats, and above six hundred scaling-ladders for storming the ramparts. The Maid Jeanne, who was nowise as the Burgundians believed, but lived a pious life and guarded her chastity, set foot to ground, and was the first down into a dry moat, which for that cause was easy to cross. But thereupon they found themselves exposed to the arrows and cross-bolts that rained down thick and fast from the Walls. Then they had in front of them a second moat. Wherefore were the Maid and her men-at-arms sore hampered. Jeanne sounded the great moat with her lance and shouted to throw in faggots.

Inside the town could be heard the roar of cannon, and all along the streets the citizens were running, half accoutred, to their posts on the ramparts, knocking over as they went

BROTHER JOCONDE

the brats playing about in the gutters. The chains were drawn across the roadways, and barricades were begun. Tribulation and tumult filled all the place.

But neither the Brother Joconde nor his Penitents saw aught of it, forasmuch as they took heed only of eternal things, and deemed the vain agitation of men to be but a foolish game. They marched through the streets singing the "Veni creator spiritus," and crying out: "Pray, for the times are at hand."

Thus they made their way in good array down the Rue Saint-Antoine, which was densely crowded with men, women, and children. Coming presently to the Place Baudet, Brother Joconde pushed through the throng and mounted a great stone that stood at the door of the Hôtel de la Truie, which Messire Florimont Lecocq, the master of the house, used to help him mount his mule. This Messire Florimont Lecocq was Sergeant at the Châtelet Prison and a partisan of the English.

So, standing on the great stone, Brother Joconde preached to the people. "Sow ye," he cried, "sow ye, good folk; sow abundantly of beans, for He which is to come will come quickly."

By the beans they were to sow, the good Brother signified the charitable works it behoved them accomplish before Our Lord should come, in the clouds of heaven, to judge both the quick and the dead. And it was urgent to sow these works without tarrying, for that the harvest would be soon. Guillaumette Dyonis, Simone la Bardine, Jeanne Chastenier, Opportune Jadoin, and Robin the gardener, stood in a ring about the Preacher, and cried "Amen!"

But the citizens, who thronged behind in a great crowd, pricked up their ears and bent their brows, thinking the Monk was foretelling the entry of Charles of Valois into his good town of Paris, over which he was fain — at any rate, so they believed — to drive the ploughshare.

Meanwhile the good Brother went on with his soul-awakening discourse.

"Oh! ye men of Paris, ye are worse than the Pagans of old Rome."

Just then the mangonels firing from the Porte Saint-Denis mingled their thunder with Brother Joconde's voice and shook the bystanders' hearts within them. Some one in the press cried out, "Death! death to traitors!"

All this time Messire Florimont Lecocq was within-doors doing on his armour. He now came forth at the noise, before he had buckled his leg-pieces. Seeing the Monk standing on his mounting-block, he asked:

"What is this good Father saying?"

And a chorus of voices answered:

"Telling us that Messire Charles of Valois is going to enter the city," while others cried:

"He is against the folk of Paris," and others again:

"He would fain cozen and betray us, like the Brother Richard, who at this very time is riding with our enemies."

But Brother Joconde made answer:

"There be neither Armagnacs, nor Burgundians, nor French, nor English, but only the sons of light and the sons of darkness. Ye are lewd fellows and your women wantons."

"Go to, thou apostate! thou sorcerer! thou traitor!" yelled Messire Florimont Lecocq, — and lugging out his sword, he plunged it in the good Brother's bosom.

With pale lips and faltering voice, the man of God still managed to say:

"Pray, fast, do penance, and ye shall be forgiven, my brethren . . ."

Then his voice choked, as the blood poured from his mouth, and he fell on the stones. Two knights, Sir John Stewart and Sir George Morris, threw themselves on the body and pierced it with more than a hundred dagger thrusts, vociferating:

"Long life to King Henry! Long life to my Lord the Duke of Bedford! Down with the Dauphin! Down with the mad Maid of the Armagnacs! Up, up! To the Gates, to the Gates!"

Therewith they ran to the Walls, drawing off with them Messire Florimont and the crowd of citizens.

Meanwhile the holy women and the gardener tarried about the bleeding corse. Simone la Bardine lay prostrate on the ground,

BROTHER JOCONDE

kissing the good Brother's feet and wiping away his blood with her unbound hair.

But Guillaumette Dyonis, standing up with her arms lifted to heaven, cried in a voice as clear as the sound of bells:

"My sisters, Jeanne, Opportune and Simone, and you, my brother, Robin the gardener, let us be going, for the times are at hand. The soul of this good Father holds me by the hand, and it will lead me aright. Wherefore ye must follow along with me. And we will say to those who are making cruel war upon each other: 'Kiss and make peace. And if ye must needs use your arms, take up the cross and go forth all together to fight the Saracens.' Come! my sisters and my brother."

Jeanne Chastenier picked up the shaft of an arrow from the ground, brake it, and made a cross, which she laid on good Brother Joconde's bosom. Then these holy women, and the gardener with them, followed after Guillaumette Dyonis, who led them by the streets and squares and alleys as if her eyes had seen the light of day. They reached the foot of the rampart, and by the stairway of a tower that was left unguarded, they mounted onto the curtain-wall. There had been no time to furnish it with its hoardings of wood; so they went along in the open. They proceeded toward the Porte Saint-Honoré, by this time enveloped in clouds of dust and smoke. It was there the Maréchal de Rais and his men were making assault. Their bolts flew thick and fast against the ramparts, and they were hurling faggots into the water of the great moat. On the hog's-back parting the great moat from the little, stood the Maid, crying: "Yield, yield you to the King of France." The English had abandoned the top of the wall in terror, leaving their dead and wounded behind them. Guillaumette Dyonis walked first, her head high and her left arm extended before her, while with her right hand she kept signing herself reverently. Simone la Bardine followed close on her heels. Then came Jeanne Chastenier and Opportune Jadoin. Robin the gardener brought up the rear, his body all shaking with his infirmity, and showing the divine stigmata on his hands. They were singing canticles as they walked.

And Guillaumette, turning now toward the city and now toward the open country, cried: "Brethren, embrace ye one another. Live in peace and harmony. Take the iron of your spearheads and forge it into ploughshares!"

Scarce had she spoken ere a shower of arrows, some from the parapet-way where a Company of Citizens was defiling, some from the hog's-back where the Armagnac men-at-arms were massed, flew in her direction, and therewith a storm of insults:

"Wanton! traitress! witch!"

Meanwhile she went on exhorting the two sides to stablish the Kingdom of Jesus Christ upon earth and to live in innocency and brotherly love, till a cross-bow bolt struck her in the throat and she staggered and fell backward.

It was which could laugh the louder at this, Armagnacs or Burgundians. Drawing her gown over her feet, she lay still and made no other stir, but gave up her soul, sighing the name of Jesus. Her eyes, which remained open, glowed like two opals.

Short while after the death of Guillaumette Dyonis the men of Paris returned in great force to man their Wall, and defended their city right valorously. Jeanne the Maid was wounded by a cross-bow bolt in the leg, and Messire Charles of Valois' men-at-arms fell back upon the Chapelle Saint-Denis. What became of Jeanne Chastenier and Opportune Jadoin no one knows. They were never heard of more. Simone la Bardine and Robin the gardener were taken the same day by the citizens on guard at the Walls and handed over to the Bishop's officer, who duly brought them before the Courts. The Church adjudged Simone heretic, and condemned her for salutary penance to the bread of suffering and the water of affliction. Robin was convicted of sorcery, and, persevering in his error, was burned alive in the Place du Parvis.

FIVE FAIR LADIES
OF PICARDY, OF POITOU, OF TOURAINE, OF LYONS, AND OF PARIS

FIVE FAIR LADIES

OF PICARDY, OF POITOU, OF TOURAINE, OF LYONS, AND OF PARIS

ONE day the Capuchin, Brother Jean Chavaray, meeting my good master the Abbé Coignard in the cloister of "The Innocents," fell into talk with him of the Brother Olivier Maillard, whose sermons, edifying and macaronic, he had lately been reading.

"There are good bits to be found in these sermons," said the Capuchin, "notably the tale of the five ladies and the go-between . . ." You will readily understand that Brother Olivier, who lived in the reign of Louis XI and whose language smacks of the coarseness of that age, uses a different word. But our century demands a certain politeness and decency in speech; wherefore I employ the term I have, to wit, *go-between.*

"You mean," replied my good master, "to signify by the expression a woman who is so obliging as to play intermediary in matters of love and love-making. The Latin has several names for her, — as *lena, conciliatrix,* also *internuntia libidinum,* ambassadress of naughty desires. These prudish dames perform the best of services; but seeing they busy themselves therein for money, we distrust their disinterestedness. Call yours a *procuress,* good Father, and have done with it; 'tis a word in common use, and has a not unseemly sound."

"So I will, Monsieur l'Abbé," assented Brother Jean Chavaray. "Only don't say *mine,* I pray, but the Brother Olivier's. A procuress then, who lived on the Pont des Tournelles, was visited one day by a knight, who put a ring into her hands. 'It is of fine gold,' he told her, 'and hath a balass ruby mounted in the bezel. An you know any dames of good estate, go say to the most comely of them that the ring is hers if she is willing to come to see me and do at my pleasure.'

"The procuress knew, by having seen them

at Mass, five ladies of an excellent beauty, — natives the first of Picardy, the second of Poitou, the third of Touraine, another from the good city of Lyons, and the last a Parisian, all dwelling in the Cité or its near neighbourhood.

"She knocked first at the Picard lady's door. A maid opened, but her mistress refused to have one word to say to her visitor. She was an honest woman.

"The procuress went next to see the lady of Poitiers and solicit her favours for the gallant knight. This dame answered her:

"'Prithee, go tell him who sent you that he is come to the wrong house, and that I am not the woman he takes me for.'

"She too is an honest woman; yet less honest than the first, in that she tried to appear more so.

"The procuress then went to see the lady from Tours, made the same offer to her as to the other, and showed her the ring.

"'I' faith,' said the lady, 'but the ring is right lovely.'

"''T is yours, an you will have it.'

"'I will not have it at the price you set on it. My husband might catch me, and I should be doing him a grief he doth not deserve.'

"This lady of Touraine is a harlot, I trow, at bottom of her heart.

"The procuress left her and went straight to the dame of Lyons, who cried:

"'Alack! my good friend, my husband is a jealous wight, and he would cut the nose off my face to hinder me winning any more rings at this pretty tilting.'

"This dame of Lyons, I tell you, is a worthless good-for-naught.

"Last of all the procuress hurried to the Parisian's. She was a hussy, and answered brazenly:

"'My husband goes Wednesday to his vineyards; tell the good sir who sent you I will come that day and see him.'

"Such, according to Brother Olivier, from Picardy to Paris, are the degrees from good to evil amongst women. What think you of the matter, Monsieur Coignard?"

To which my good master made answer:

" 'T is a shrewd matter to consider the acts and impulses of these petty creatures in their relations with Eternal Justice. I have no lights thereanent. But methinks the Lyons dame who feared having her nose cut off was a more good-for-nothing baggage than the Parisian who was afraid of nothing."

"I am far, very far, from allowing it," replied Brother Jean Chavaray. "A woman who fears her husband may come to fear hell fire. Her Confessor, it may be, will bring her to do penance and give alms. For, after all, that is the end we must come at. But what can a poor Capuchin hope to get of a woman whom *nothing* terrifies?"

A GOOD LESSON WELL LEARNT

A GOOD LESSON WELL LEARNT

IN the days of King Louis XI there lived at Paris, in a matted chamber, a citizen dame called Violante, who was comely and well-liking in all her person. She had so bright a face that Master Jacques Tribouillard, doctor in law and a renowned cosmographer, who was often a visitor at her house, was used to tell her:

"Seeing you, madame, I deem credible and even hold it proven, what Cucurbitus Piger lays down in one of his scholia on Strabo, to wit, that the famous city and university of Paris was of old known by the name of Lutetia or Leucecia, or some suchlike word coming from *Leuké*, that is to say, 'the white,' forasmuch as the ladies of the same had bosoms white as snow,—yet not so clear and bright and white as is your own, madame."

To which Violante would say in answer:

"'T is enough for me if my bosom is not fit to fright folks, like some I wot of. And, if I show it, why, 't is to follow the fashion. I have not the hardihood to do otherwise than the rest of the world."

Now Madame Violante had been wedded, in the flower of her youth, to an Advocate of the Parlement, a man of a harsh temper and sorely set on the arraignment and punishing of unfortunate prisoners. For the rest, he was of sickly habit and a weakling, of such a sort he seemed more fit to give pain to folks outside his doors than pleasure to his wife within. The old fellow thought more of his blue bags than of his better half, though these were far otherwise shapen, being bulgy and fat and formless. But the lawyer spent his nights over them.

Madame Violante was too reasonable a woman to love a husband that was so unlovable. Master Jacques Tribouillard upheld she was a good wife, as steadfastly and surely confirmed and stablished in conjugal virtue as Lucretia the Roman. And for proof he alleged that he had altogether failed to turn her aside from the path of honour. The judicious observed a prudent silence on the point, holding that what is hid will only be made manifest at the last Judgment Day. They noted how the lady was over fond of gewgaws and laces and wore in company and at church gowns of velvet and silk and cloth of gold, purfled with miniver; but they were too fair-minded folk to decide whether, damning as she did Christian men who saw her so comely and so finely dressed to the torments of vain longing, she was not damning her own soul too with one of them. In a word, they were well ready to stake Madame Violante's virtue on the toss of a coin, cross or pile,—which is greatly to the honour of that fair lady.

The truth is her Confessor, Brother Jean Turelure, was for ever upbraiding her.

"Think you, madame," he would ask her, "that the blessed St. Catherine won heaven by leading such a life as yours, baring her bosom and sending to Genoa for lace ruffles?"

But he was a great preacher, very severe on human weaknesses, who could condone naught and thought he had done everything when he had inspired terror. He threatened her with hell fire for having washed her face with ass's milk.

As a fact, no one could say if she had given her old husband a meet and proper head-dress, and Messire Philippe de Coetquis used to warn the honest dame in a merry vein:

"See to it, I say! He is bald, he will catch his death of cold!"

Messire Philippe de Coetquis was a knight of gallant bearing, as handsome as the knave of hearts in the noble game of cards. He had first encountered Madame Violante one evening at a ball, and after dancing with her far into the night, had carried her home on his crupper, while the Advocate splashed his way through the mud and mire of the kennels by the dancing light of the torches his four tipsy lackeys bore. In the course of these merry doings, a-foot and on horseback, Messire Philippe de Coetquis had formed a shrewd notion that Madame Violante had a limber waist and a full, firm bosom of her own, and there and then had been smit by her charms.

He was a frank and guileless wight and made bold to tell her outright what he would have of her,—to wit, to hold her naked in his two arms.

To which she would make answer:

"Messire Philippe, you know not what you say. I am a virtuous wife,"—

Or another time:

"Messire Philippe, come back again to-morrow,—"

And when he came next day she would ask innocently:

"Nay, where is the hurry?"

These never-ending postponements caused the Chevalier no little distress and chagrin. He was ready to believe, with Master Tribouillard, that Madame Violante was indeed a Lucretia, so true is it that all men are alike in fatuous self-conceit! And we are bound to say she had not so much as suffered him to kiss her mouth,—only a pretty diversion after all and a bit of wanton playfulness.

Things were in this case when Brother Jean Turelure was called to Venice by the General of his Order, to preach to sundry Turks lately converted to the true Faith.

Before setting forth, the good Brother went to take leave of his fair Penitent, and upbraided her with more than usual sternness for living a dissolute life. He exhorted her urgently to repent and pressed her to wear a hair-shirt next her skin, — an incomparable remedy against naughty cravings and a sovran medicine for natures over prone to the sins of the flesh.

She besought him: "Good Brother, never ask too much of me."

But he would not hearken, and threatened her with the pains of hell if she did not amend her ways. Then he told her he would gladly execute any commissions she might be pleased to entrust him with. He was in hopes she would beg him to bring her back some consecrated medal, a rosary, or, better still, a little of the soil of the Holy Sepulchre which the Turks carry from Jerusalem together with dried roses, and which the Italian monks sell.

But Madame Violante preferred a quite other request:

"Good Brother, dear Brother, as you are going to Venice, where such cunning workmen in this sort are to be found, I pray you bring me back a Venetian mirror, the clearest and truest can be gotten."

Brother Jean Turelure promised to content her wish.

While her Confessor was abroad, Madame Violante led the same life as before. And when Messire Philippe pressed her: "Were it not well to take our pleasure together?" she would answer: "Nay! 'tis too hot. Look at the weathercock if the wind will not change anon." And the good folk who watched her ways were in despair of her ever giving a proper pair of horns to her crabbed old husband. "'Tis a sin and a shame!" they declared.

On his return from Italy Brother Jean Turelure presented himself before Madame Violante and told her he had brought what she desired.

"Look, madame," he said, and drew from under his gown a death's-head.

"Here, madame, is your mirror. This death's-head was given me for that of the prettiest woman in all Venice. She was what you are, and you will be much like her anon."

Madame Violante, mastering her surprise and horror, answered the good Father in a well-assured voice that she understood the lesson he would teach her and she would not fail to profit thereby.

"I shall aye have present in my mind, good Brother, the mirror you have brought me from Venice, wherein I see my likeness not as I am at present, but as doubtless I soon shall be. I promise you to govern my behaviour by this salutary thought."

Brother Jean Turelure was far from expecting such pious words. He expressed some satisfaction.

"So, madame," he murmured, "you see yourself the need of altering your ways. You promise me henceforth to govern your behaviour by the thought this fleshless skull hath brought home to you. Will you not make the same promise to God as you have to me?"

She asked if indeed she must, and he assured her it behoved her so to do.

A GOOD LESSON WELL LEARNT

"Well, I will give this promise then," she declared.

"Madame, this is very well. There is no going back on your word now."

"I shall not go back on it, never fear."

Having won this binding promise, Brother Jean Turelure left the place, radiant with satisfaction. And as he went from the house, he cried out loud in the street:

"Here is a good work done! By Our Lord God's good help, I have turned and set in the way toward the gate of Paradise a lady, who, albeit not sinning precisely in the way of fornication spoken of by the Prophet, yet was wont to employ for men's temptation the clay whereof the Creator had kneaded her that she might serve and adore him withal. She will forsake these naughty habits to adopt a better life. I have throughly changed her. Praise be to God!"

Hardly had the good Brother gone down the stairs when Messire Philippe de Coetquis ran up them and scratched at Madame Violante's door. She welcomed him with a beaming smile, and led him into a closet, furnished with carpets and cushions galore, wherein he had never been admitted before. From this he augured well. He offered her sweetmeats he had in a box.

"Here be sugar-plums to suck, madame; they are sweet and sugared, but not so sweet as your lips."

To which the lady retorted he was a vain, silly fop to make boast of a fruit he had never tasted.

He answered her meetly, kissing her forthwith on the mouth.

She manifested scarce any annoyance and said only she was an honest woman and a true wife. He congratulated her and advised her not to lock up this jewel of hers in such close keeping that no man could enjoy it. "For, of a surety," he swore, "you will be robbed of it, and that right soon."

"Try then," said she, cuffing him daintily over the ears with her pretty pink palms.

But he was master by this time to take whatsoever he wished of her. She kept protesting with little cries:

"I won't have it. Fie! fie on you, mes-

A GOOD LESSON WELL LEARNT 103

sire! You must not do it. Oh! sweetheart . . . oh! my love . . . my life! You are killing me!"

Anon, when she had done sighing and dying, she said sweetly:

"Messire Philippe, never flatter yourself you have mastered me by force or guile. You have had of me what you craved, but 'twas of mine own free will, and I only resisted so much as was needful that I might yield me as I liked best. Sweetheart, I am yours. If, for all your handsome face, which I loved from the first, and despite the tenderness of your wooing, I did not before grant you what you have just won with my consent, 'twas because I had no true understanding of things. I had no thought of the flight of time and the shortness of life and love; plunged in a soft languor of indolence, I reaped no harvest of my youth and beauty. However, the good Brother Jean Turelure hath given me a profitable lesson. He hath taught me the preciousness of the hours. But now he showed me a death's-head, saying: 'Suchlike you will be soon.' This taught me we must be quick to enjoy the pleasures of love and make the most of the little space of time reserved to us for that end."

These words and the caresses wherewith Madame Violante seconded them persuaded Messire Philippe to turn the time to good account, to set to work afresh to his own honour and profit and the pleasure and glory of his mistress, and to multiply the sure proofs of prowess which it behoves every good and loyal servant to give on suchlike an occasion.

After which, she was ready to cry quits. Taking him by the hand, she guided him back to the door, kissed him daintily on the eyes, and asked:

"Sweetheart Philippe, is it not well done to follow the precepts of the good Brother Jean Turelure?"

SATAN'S TONGUE-PIE

SATAN'S TONGUE–PIE

ATAN lay in his bed with the flaming curtains. The physicians and apothecaries of Hell, finding their patient had a white tongue, inferred he was suffering from a weakness of the stomach and prescribed a diet at once light and nourishing.

Satan swore he had no appetite for aught but a certain earthly dish, which women excel in making when they meet in company, to wit, tongue-pie.

The doctors agreed there was nothing could better suit His Majesty's stomach.

In an hour's time the dish was set before the King; but he found it insipid and tasteless.

He sent for his Head Cook and asked him where the pie came from.

"From Paris, sire. It is quite fresh; 'twas baked this very morning, in the Marais

Quarter, by a dozen gossips gathered round the bed at a woman's lying-in."

"Ah! now I know the reason it is so flavourless," returned the Prince of Darkness. "You have not been to the best cooks for dishes of the sort. Citizens' wives, they do their best; but they lack delicacy, they lack the fine touch of genius. Women of the people are clumsier still. For a real good tongue-pie a Nunnery is the place to go to. There's nobody to match these old maids of Religion for a pretty skill in compounding all the needful ingredients,—fine spices of rancour, thyme of backbiting, fennel of insinuation, bay-leaf of calumny."

This parable is taken from a sermon of the good Father Gillotin Landoulle, a poor, unworthy Capuchin.

CONCERNING AN
HORRIBLE PICTURE

CONCERNING AN

HORRIBLE PICTURE

THE WHICH WAS SHOWED IN A TEMPLE AND OF SUNDRY LIMNINGS OF A RIGHT PACIFIC AND AMOROUS SORT THE WHICH THE SAGE PHILEMON HAD HANGED IN HIS LIBRARIE AND OF A NOBLE PORTRAITURE OF THE POET HOMER THE WHICH THE AFORESAID PHILEMON DID PRIZE ABOVE ALL OTHER LIMNINGS

PHILEMON was used to confess how, in the fire of his callow youth and fine flower of his lustie springal days, he had been stung with murderous frenzie at view of a certaine picture of Apelles, the which in those times was showed in a temple. And the said picture did present Alexander the Great laying on right shrewdly at Darius, king of the Indians, whiles round about these twain, soldiers and captains were a-slaying one another with a savage furie and in divers strange fashions. And the said work was right cun-

ningly wrought and in very close mimicrie of nature. And none, an they were in the hot and lustie season of their life, could cast a look thereon without being stirred incontinent to be striking and killing poor harmlesse folk for the sole sake of donning so rich an harnesse and bestriding such high-stepping chargers as did these good codpieces in their battle, — for that young blood doth aye take pleasure in horseflesh and the practise of arms. This had the aforesaid Philemon proven in his day. And he was used to say how ever after 'twas his wont to turn aside his eyen of set purpose from suchlike pictures of wars and bloodshed, and that he did so heartily loathe these cruelties as that he could not abear to behold them even set forth in counterfeit presentment.

And he was used to say that any honest and prudent wight must needs be sore offended and scandalized by all this appalling array of armour and bucklers and the horde of warriors Homer calls *Corythaioloi* (glancing-helmed) by reason of the terrifying hideousness of their head-gear, and that the portrayal of these same fighting fellows was in very truth unseemly, as

AN HORRIBLE PICTURE

contrarie to good and peaceable manners, immodest, no thing in the world being more shameful then homicide, and eke lascivious, as alluring folk to cruelty, the which is the worst of all allurements. For to entice to pleasant dalliaunce is a far lesse heinous fault.

And the aforesaid Philemon was used to say that it was honest, decent, of good ensample and entirely modest to show by painting, chiselling, or any other fine artifice the scenes of the Golden Age, to wit maidens and young men interlacing limbs in accord with the craving of kindly Nature, or other the like delectable fancy, as of a Nymph lying laughing in the grass. And on her ripe smiling mouth a Faun is crushing a purple grape.

And he was used to say that belike the Golden Age had never flourished save only in the fond imagining of the poets, and that our first forebears of human kind, being yet barbarous and silly folk, had known naught at all thereof; but that, an the said age could not credibly be deemed to have been at the beginning of the world, we might well wish it should be at the end, and that meanwhiles it was a gracious boon to offer us a likeness of the same in pictured image.

And like as it is (so he would say) obscene, — 't is the word Virgil writes of dogs wallowing in the mud and mire, — to depict murderers, whoreson men-at arms, fighting-men, conquering heroes and plundering thieves, wreaking their foul and wicked will, yea! and poor devils licking the dust and swallowing the same in great mouthfuls, and one unhappie wretch that hath been felled to the earth and is striving to get to his feet againe, but is pinned down by an horse's hoof pressing on his chops, and another that looketh piteously about him for that his pennon hath been shorn from him and his hand with it, — so is it of right subtile and so to say heavenly art to exhibit prettie blandishments, caresses, frolickings, beauties and delights, and the loves of the Nymphs and Fauns in the woods. And he would have it there was none offence in these naked bodies, clothed upon enow with their owne grace and comeliness.

And he had in his closet, this same Philemon aforesaid, a very marvellous painting, wherein was limned a young Faun in act to filch away

AN HORRIBLE PICTURE

with a craftie hand a light cloth did cover the belly of a sleeping Nymph. 'Twas plain to see he was full fain of his freak and seemed to be saying: The body of this young goddess is so sweet and refreshing as that the fountaine springing in the shade of the woods is not more delightsome. How I do love to look upon you, soft sweet lap, and prettie white thighs, and shady cavern at once terrifying and entrancing! And over the heads of the twain did hover winged Cupids and watched them laughingly, whiles fair dames and their gallants, their brows wreathen with flowers, footed it on the lush grass.

And he had, the aforesaid Philemon, yet other limnings of cunning craftsmanship in his closet. And he did prize very high the portraiture of a good doctor a-sitting in his cabinet writing at a table by candle-light. The said cabinet was fully furnished with globes, gnomons, and astrolabes, proper for meting the movements of the orbs of heaven, the which is a right praiseworthy task and one that doth lift the spirit to sublime thoughts and the exceeding pure love of Venus Urania.

And there was hanging from the joists of the said cabinet a great serpent and crocodile, forasmuch as they be rarities and very needful for the due understanding of anatomy. And he had likewise, the said doctor, amid his belongings, the books of the most excellent philosophers of Antiquity and eke the treatises of Hippocrates. And he was an ensample to young men which should be fain, by hard swinking, to stuff their pates with as much high learning and occult lore as he had under his own bonnet.

And he had, the aforesaid Philemon, painted on a panel that shined like a polished mirror a portraiture of Homer in the guise of an old blind man, his beard white as the flowers of the hawthorn and his temples bound about with the fillets sacred to the god Apollo, which had loved him above all other men. And, to look at that good old man, you deemed verily his lips were presently to ope and break into words of melodie.

MADEMOISELLE DE DOU-
CINE'S NEW YEAR'S
PRESENT

MADEMOISELLE DE DOUCINE'S NEW YEAR'S PRESENT

ON January 1st, in the forenoon, the good M. Chanterelle sallied out on foot from his hôtel in the Faubourg Saint-Marcel. He felt the cold and was a poor walker; so it was a real penance to him to face the chilly air and the bleak streets which were full of half-melted snow. He had refused to take his coach by way of mortifying the flesh, having grown very solicitous since his illness about the salvation of his soul. He lived in retirement, aloof from all society and company, and paid no visits save to his niece, Mademoiselle de Doucine, a little girl of seven.

Leaning on his walking-cane, he made his way painfully to the Rue Saint-Honoré and entered the shop of Madame Pinson at the sign of the *Panier Fleuri*. Here was displayed an abundant stock of children's toys to tempt customers seeking presents for this New Year's Day of 1696. You could scarce move for the host of mechanical figures of dancers and tipplers, birds in the bush that clapped their wings and sang, cabinets full of wax puppets, soldiers in white and blue ranged in battle array, and dolls dressed some as fine ladies, others as servant wenches, for the inequality of stations, established by God himself among mankind, appeared even in these innocent mannikins.

M. Chanterelle chose a doll. The one he selected was dressed like the Princess of Savoy on her arrival in France, on November 4th. The head was a mass of bows and ribbons; she wore a very stiff corsage, covered with gold filigrees, and a brocade petticoat with an overskirt caught up by pearl clasps.

M. Chanterelle smiled to think of the delight such a lovely doll would give Mademoiselle de Doucine, and when Madame Pinson handed him the Princess of Savoy wrapped up in silk paper, a gleam of sensuous satisfaction flitted over his kind face, pinched as it was with illness, pale with fasting and haggard with the fear of hell.

He thanked Madame Pinson courteously, clapped the Princess under his arm and walked away, dragging his leg painfully, towards the house where he knew Mademoiselle de Doucine was waiting for him to attend her morning levée.

At the corner of the Rue de l'Arbre-Sec, he met M. Spon, whose great nose dived almost into his lace cravat.

"Good morning, Monsieur Spon," he greeted him. "I wish you a happy New Year, and I pray God everything may turn out according to your wishes."

"Oh! my good sir, don't say that," cried M. Spon. "'Tis often for our chastisement that God grants our wishes. *Et tribuit eis petitionem eorum.*"

"'Tis very true," returned M. Chanterelle, "we do not know our own best interests. I am an example myself, as I stand before you. I thought at first that the complaint I have suffered from for the last two years was a curse; but I see now it is a blessing, since it has removed me from the abominable life I was leading at the play-houses and in society. This complaint, which tortures my limbs and is like to turn my brain, is a signal token of God's goodness toward me. But, sir, will you not do me the favour to accompany me as far as the Rue du Roule, whither I am bound, to carry a New Year's gift to my niece Mademoiselle de Doucine?"

At the words M. Spon threw up his arms and gave a great cry of horror.

"What!" he exclaimed. "Can it be M. Chanterelle I hear say such things,— and not some profligate libertine? Is it possible, sir, that living as you do a religious and retired life, I see you all in a moment plunge into the vices of the day?"

"Alack! I did not think I was plunging into vice," faltered M. Chanterelle, trembling all over. "But I sorely lack a lamp of guidance. Is it so great a sin then to offer a doll to Mademoiselle de Doucine?"

"Yes, a great and terrible sin," replied M. Spon. "And what you are offering this innocent child to-day is meeter to be called an

MADEMOISELLE'S PRESENT

idol, a devilish simulacrum, than a doll. Are you not aware, sir, that the custom of New Year's gifts is a foul superstition and a hideous survival of Paganism?"

"No, I did not know that," said M. Chanterelle.

"Let me tell you, then," resumed M. Spon, "that this custom descends from the Romans, who seeing something divine in all beginnings, held the beginning of the year holy also. Hence, to act as they did is to do idolatry. You make New Year's offerings, sir, in imitation of the worshippers of the God Janus. Be consistent, and like them consecrate to Juno the first day of every month."

M. Chanterelle, hardly able to keep his feet, begged M. Spon to give him his arm, and while they moved on, M. Spon proceeded in the same vein:

"Is it because the Astrologers have fixed on the first of January for the beginning of the year that you deem yourself obliged to make presents on that day? Pray, what call have you to revive at that precise date the affection of your friends. Was their love dying then with the dying year? And will it be so much worth the having when you have reanimated it by dint of cajolements and baneful gifts?"

"Sir," returned the good M. Chanterelle, leaning on M. Spon's arm and trying hard to make his tottering steps keep pace with his impetuous companion's, "sir, before my sickness, I was only a miserable sinner, taking no heed but to treat my friends with civility and govern my behaviour by the principles of honesty and honour. Providence hath deigned to rescue me from this abyss, and I direct my conduct since my conversion by the admonitions the Director of my conscience gives me. But I have been so light-minded and thoughtless as not to seek his advice on this question of New Year's gifts. What you tell me of them, sir, with the authority of a man alike admirable for sober living and sound doctrine, amazes and confounds me."

"Nay! that is indeed what I mean to do," resumed M. Spon,—"to confound you, and to illumine you, not indeed by my own lights, which burn feebly, but by those of a great Doctor. Sit you down on that wayside post."

MADEMOISELLE'S PRESENT

And pushing M. Chanterelle into the archway of a carriage gate, where he made himself as easy as circumstances allowed, M. Spon drew from his pocket a little parchment-bound book, which he opened, and after hunting through the pages, lighted on a passage which he proceeded to read out loud amid a gaping circle of chimney-sweeps, chamber-maids, and scullions who had collected at the resounding tones of his voice:

"'We who hold in abhorrence the festivals of the Jews, and who would deem strange and outlandish their Sabbaths and New Moons and other Holy Days erst loved of the Almighty, we deal familiarly with the Saturnalia and the Calends of January, with the Matronalia and the Feast of the Winter Solstice; New Year's gifts and foolish presents fill all our thoughts; merrymakings and junketings are in every house. The Heathens guard their religion better; they are heedful to observe none of our Feasts, for fear of being taken for Christians, while we never hesitate to make ourselves look like Heathens by celebrating their Ceremonial Days.'

"You hear what I say," went on M. Spon. "'T is Tertullian speaks in this wise and from the depths of Africa displays before your eyes, sir, the odiousness of your behaviour. He it is upbraids you, declaring how 'New Year's gifts and foolish presents fill all your thoughts. You keep holy the feasts of the Heathen.' I have not the honour to know your Confessor. But I shudder, sir, to think of the way he neglects his duty toward you. Tell me this, can you rest assured that at the day of your death, when you come to stand before God, he will be at your side, to take upon him the sins he hath suffered you to fall into?"

After haranguing in this sort, he put back his book in his pocket and marched off with angry strides, followed at a distance by the astonished chimney-sweeps and scullions.

The good M. Chanterelle was left sitting alone on his post with the Princess of Savoy, and thinking how he was risking the eternal pains of hell fire for giving a doll to Mademoiselle de Doucine, his niece, he fell to pondering the unfathomable mysteries of Religion.

His legs, which had been tottery for several

months, refused to carry him, and he felt as unhappy as ever a well-meaning man possibly can in this world.

He had been sitting stranded in this distressful mood on his post for some minutes when a Capuchin friar stepped up and addressed him:

"Sir, will you not give New Year's presents to the Little Brethren who are poor, for the love of God?"

"Why! what! good Father," M. Chanterelle burst out, "you are a man of religion, and you ask me for New Year's gifts?"

"Sir," replied the Capuchin, "the good St. Francis bade his sons make merry with all simplicity. Give the Capuchins wherewith to make a good meal this day, that they may endure with cheerfulness the abstinence and fasting they must observe all the rest of the year,—barring, of course, Sundays and Feast Days."

M. Chanterelle gazed at the holy man with wonder:

"Are you not afraid, Father, that this custom of New Year's gifts is baneful to the soul?"

"No, I am not afraid."

"The custom comes to us from the Pagans."

"The Pagans sometimes followed good customs. God was pleased to suffer some faint rays of his light to pierce the darkness of the Gentiles. Sir, if you refuse to give *us* presents, never refuse a boon to our poor little ones. We have a home for foundlings. With this poor crown I shall buy each child a little paper windmill and a cake. They will owe you the only pleasure perhaps of all their life; for they are not fated to have much joy in the world. Their laughter will go up to heaven; when children laugh, they praise the Lord."

M. Chanterelle laid his well-filled purse in the poor friar's palm and got him down from his post, saying over softly to himself the word he had just heard:

"When children laugh, they praise the Lord."

Then his soul was comforted and he marched off with a firmer step to carry the Princess of Savoy to Mademoiselle de Doucine, his niece.

MADEMOISELLE ROXANE

MADEMOISELLE ROXANE

Y good master, M. l'Abbé Coignard, had taken me with him to sup with one of his old fellow-students, who lodged in a garret in the Rue Gît-le-Cœur. Our host, a Premonstratensian Father of much learning and a fine Theologian, had fallen out with the Prior of his House for having writ a little book relating the calamities of Mam'zelle Fanchon. The end of it was he turned tavern-keeper at The Hague. He was now returned to France and living precariously by the sermons he composed, which were full of high argument and eloquence. After supper he had read us these same calamities of Mam'zelle Fanchon, source of his own, and the reading had kept us there till a late hour. At last I found myself without-doors with my good master, under a wondrous fine

summer's night, which made me straightway comprehend the verity of the ancient fables regarding the loves of Diana and feel how natural it is to employ in soft dalliance the silent, silvery hours of night. I said as much to M. l'Abbé Coignard, who retorted that love is to blame for many and great ills.

"Tournebroche, my son," he asked me, "have you not just heard from the mouth of yonder good Monk how, for having loved a recruiting sergeant, a clerk of M. Gaulot's mercer at the sign of the Truie-qui-file, and the younger son of M. le Lieutenant-Criminel Leblanc, Mam'zelle Fanchon was clapped in hospital? Would you wish to be any of these, — sergeant or clerk or limb of the law?"

I answered I would indeed. My good master thanked me for my candid avowal, and quoted some verses of Lucretius to persuade me that love is contrary to the tranquillity of a truly philosophical soul.

Thus discoursing, we were come to the round-point of the Pont-Neuf. Leaning our elbows on the parapet, we looked over at the great tower of the Châtelet, which stood out black in the moonlight.

"There might be much to say," sighed my good master, "on this justice of the civilized nations, the punishments whereof in retaliation are often more cruel than the crime itself. I cannot believe that these tortures and penalties that men inflict on their fellows are necessary for the safeguarding of States, seeing how from time to time one and another legal cruelty is done away with without hurt to the commonweal. And I hold it likely that the severities they still maintain are no whit more useful than those they have abolished. But men are cruel. Come away, Tournebroche, my dear lad; it grieves me to think how unhappy prisoners are even now lying awake behind those walls in anguish and despair. I know they have done faultily, but this doth not hinder me from pitying them. Which of us is without offence?"

We went on our way. The bridge was deserted save for a beggarman and woman, who met on the causeway. The pair drew stealthily into one of the recesses over the piers, where they lurked together on the door-step of a huckster's booth. They seemed well enough content, both of them, to mingle their joint wretchedness, and when we went by were thinking of quite other things than craving our charity. Nevertheless my good master, who was the most compassionate of men, threw them a half farthing, the last piece of money left in his breeches pocket.

"They will pick up our obol," he said, "when they have come back to the consciousness of their misery. I pray they may not quarrel then over fiercely for possession of the coin."

We passed on without further rencounter till on the Quai des Oiseleurs we espied a young damsel striding along with a notable air of resolution. Hastening our pace to get a nearer view, we saw she had a slim waist and fair hair in which the moonbeams played prettily. She was dressed like a citizen's wife or daughter.

"There goes a pretty girl," said the Abbé; "how comes it she is out of doors alone at this hour of night?"

MADEMOISELLE ROXANE

"Truly," I agreed, "'t is not the sort one generally encounters on the bridges after curfew."

Our surprise was changed to alarm when we saw her go down to the river bank by a little stairway the sailors use. We ran towards her; but she did not seem to hear us. She halted at the edge; the stream was running high, and the dull roar of the swollen waters could be heard some way off. She stood a moment motionless, her head thrown back and arms hanging, in an attitude of despair. Then, bending her graceful neck, she put her two hands over her face and kept it hid behind her fingers for some seconds. Next moment she suddenly grasped her skirts and dragged them forward with the gesture a woman always uses when she is going to jump. My good master and I came up with her just as she was taking the fatal leap, and we hauled her forcibly backward. She struggled to get free of our arms; and as the bank was all slimy and slippery with ooze deposited by the receding waters (for the river was already beginning to fall), M.

l'Abbé Coignard came very near being dragged in too. I was losing my foothold myself. But as luck would have it, my feet lighted on a root which held me up as I crouched there with my arms round the best of masters and this despairing young thing. Presently, coming to the end of her strength and courage, she fell back on M. l'Abbé Coignard's breast, and we managed all three to scramble to the top of the bank again. He helped her up daintily, with a certain easy grace that was always his. Then he led the way to a great beech-tree at the foot of which was a wooden bench, on which he seated her.

Taking his place beside her:

"Mademoiselle," he said gently, "you need have no fear. Say nothing just yet, but be assured it is a friend sits by you."

Next, turning to me, my master went on:

"Tournebroche, my son, we may congratulate ourselves on having brought this strange adventure to a good end. But I have left my hat down yonder on the river bank; albeit it has lost pretty near all its lace and is threadbare with long service, it was still good to guard my old head, sorely tried by years and labours, against sun and rain. Go see, my son, if it may still be found where I dropped it. And if you discover it, bring it me, I beg,—likewise one of my shoe buckles, which I see I have lost. For my part I will stay by this damsel we have rescued and watch over her slumber."

I ran back to the spot we had just quitted and was lucky enough to find my good master's hat. The buckle I could not espy anywhere. True, I did not take any very excessive pains to hunt for it, having never all my life seen my good master with more than one shoe buckle. When I returned to the tree, I found the damsel still in the same state, sitting quite motionless with her head leant against the trunk of the beech. I noticed now that she was of a very perfect beauty. She wore a silk mantle trimmed with lace, very neat and proper, and on her feet light shoes, the buckles of which caught the moonbeams.

I could not have enough of examining her. Suddenly she opened her drooping lids, and casting a look that was still misty at M. Coignard and me, she began in a feeble voice, but with the tone and accent, I thought, of a person of gentility:

"I am not ungrateful, sirs, for the service you have done me from feelings of humanity; but I cannot truthfully tell you I am glad, for the life to which you have restored me is a curse, a hateful, cruel torment."

At these sad words my good master, whose face wore a look of compassion, smiled softly, for he could not really think life was to be for ever hateful to so young and pretty a creature.

"My child," he told her, "things strike us in a totally different light according as they are near at hand or far off. It is no time for you to despair. Such as I am, and brought to this sorry plight by the buffets of time and fortune, I yet make shift to endure a life wherein my pleasures are to translate Greek and dine sometimes with sundry very worthy friends. Look at me, mademoiselle, and say, — would you consent to live in the same conditions as I?"

She looked him over; her eyes almost

laughed, and she shook her head. Then, resuming her melancholy and mournfulness, she faltered:

"There is not in all the world so unhappy a being as I am."

"Mademoiselle," returned my good master, "I am discreet both by calling and temperament; I will not seek to force your confibence. But your looks betray you; any one can see you are sick of disappointed love. Well, 't is not an incurable complaint. I have had it myself, and I have lived many a long year since then."

He took her hand, gave her a thousand tokens of his sympathy, and went on in these terms:

"There is only one thing I regret for the moment,—that I cannot offer you a refuge for the night, or what is left of it. My present lodging is in an old château a long way from here, where I am busy translating a Greek book along with young Master Tournebroche whom you see here."

My master spoke the truth. We were living at the time with M. d'Astarac, at the

Château des Sablons, in the village of Neuilly, and were in the pay of a great alchemist, who died later under tragic circumstances.

"At the same time, mademoiselle," my master added, "if you should know of any place where you think you could go, I shall be happy to escort you thither."

To which the girl answered she appreciated all his kindness, that she lived with a kinswoman, to whose house she could count on being admitted at any hour; but that she had rather not return before daylight. She was fain, she said, not to disturb quiet folks' sleep, and dreaded moreover to have her grief too painfully renewed by the sight of her old, familiar surroundings.

As she spoke thus, the tears rained down from her eyes. My good master bade her:

"Mademoiselle, give me your handkerchief, if you please, and I will wipe your eyes. Then I will take you to wait for daybreak under the archways of the Halles, where we can sit in comfort under shelter from the night dews."

The girl smiled through her tears.

"I do not like," she said, "to give you so much trouble. Go your way, sir, and rest assured you take my best thanks with you."

For all that she laid her hand on the arm my good master offered her, and we set out, all the three of us, for the Halles. The night had turned much cooler. In the sky, which was beginning to assume a milky hue, the stars were growing paler and fainter. We could hear the first of the market-gardeners' carts rumbling along to the Halles, drawn by a slow-stepping horse, half asleep in the shafts. Arrived at the archways, we chose a place in the recess of a porch distinguished by an image of St. Nicholas, and established ourselves all three on a stone step, on which M. l'Abbé Coignard took the precaution of spreading his cloak before he let his young charge sit down.

Thereupon my good master fell to discoursing on divers subjects, choosing merry and enlivening themes of set purpose to drive away the gloomy thoughts that might assail our companion's mind. He told her he accounted this rencounter the most fortunate he had ever chanced on all his life, and that he should ever cherish a fond recollection of one who had so deeply touched him, — all this, however, without ever asking to know her name and story.

My good master thought no doubt that the unknown would presently tell him what he refrained from asking. She broke into a fresh flood of weeping, heaved a deep sigh and said:

"I should be churlish, sir, to reward your kindness with silence. I am not afraid to trust myself in your hands. My name is Sophie T——. You have guessed the truth; 't is the betrayal of a lover I was too fondly attached to has brought me to despair. If you deem my grief excessive, that is because you do not know how great was my assurance, how blind my infatuation, and you cannot realize how enchanting was the paradise I have lost."

Then, raising her lovely eyes to our faces, she went on:

"Sirs, I am not such a woman as your meeting me thus at night time might lead you to suppose. My father was a merchant. He went, in the way of trade, to America, and was lost on his way home in a shipwreck, he and his merchandise with him. My mother was so overwhelmed by these calamities that she fell into a decline and died, leaving me, while still a child, to the charge of an aunt, who brought me up. I was a good girl till the hour I met the man whose love was to afford me indescribable delights, ending in the despair wherein you now see me plunged."

So saying, Sophie hid her face in her handkerchief. Presently she resumed with a sigh:

"His worldly rank was so far above my own I could never expect to be his except in secret. I flattered myself he would be faithful to me. He swore he loved me, and easily overcame my scruples. My aunt was aware of our feelings for one another, and raised no obstacles, for two reasons, — because her affection for me made her indulgent, and because my dear lover's high position impressed her imagination. I lived a year of perfect happiness only equalled by the wretchedness I now endure. This morning he came to see me at my aunt's, with whom I live. I was haunted by dark forebodings. As I dressed my hair but an hour or so before, I had broken a mirror he had given me. The sight of him only increased my misgivings, for I noticed instantly that his face wore an unaccustomed look of constraint . . . Oh! sir, was ever woman so unhappy as I ? . . ."

Her eyes filled again with tears; but she kept them back under her lids, and was able to finish her tale, which my good master deemed as touching, but by no means so unique, as she did herself.

"He informed me coldly, though not without signs of embarrassment, that his father having bought him a Company, he was leaving to join the colours. First, however, he said, his family required him to plight his troth to the daughter of an Intendant of Finances; the connection was advantageous to his fortune and would bring him means adequate to support his rank and make a figure in the world. And the traitor, never deigning to notice my pale looks, added in his soft, caressing voice which had made me so many vows of affection, that his new obligations would prevent his seeing me again, at least for some while. He assured me further that he was still my friend and begged me to accept a sum of money in memory of the days we had passed together.

"And with the words he held out a purse to me.

"I am telling you the truth, sirs, when I assure you I had always refused to listen to the offers he repeated again and again, to give me fine clothes, furniture, plate, an establishment, and to take me away from my aunt's, where I lived in very narrow circumstances, and settle me in a most elegant little mansion he had in the Rue du Roule. My wish was that we should be united only by the ties of affection, and I was proud to have of his gift nothing but a few jewels whose sole value came from the fact of his being the donor. My gorge rose at the sight of the purse he offered me, and the insult gave me strength to banish from my presence the impostor whom in one moment I had learnt to know and to despise. He faced my angry looks unabashed, and assured me with the utmost unconcern that I could know nothing of the paramount obligations that fill the existence of a man of quality, adding that he hoped eventually, when I looked at things quietly, I should come to see his behaviour in a better light. Then, returning the purse to his pocket, he declared he would readily find a way of putting the contents at my disposal in such a manner as to make it impossible for me to refuse his liberality. Thus leaving me with the odious, the intolerable implication that he was going to make full amends by these sordid means, he made for the door to which I pointed without a word. When he was gone, I felt a calmness of mind that surprised myself. It arose from the resolution I had formed to die. I dressed with some care, wrote a letter to my aunt asking her forgiveness for the pain I was about to cause her by my death, and went out into the streets. There I roamed about all the afternoon and evening and a part of the night, moving from busy thoroughfare to deserted lane without a trace of fatigue, postponing the execution of my purpose to make it more sure and certain under the favouring conditions of darkness and solitude. Possibly too I found a certain weak pleasure in dallying with the thought of dying and tasting the mournful satisfaction of my coming release from my troubles. At two o'clock in the morning, I went down to the river's brink. Sirs, you know the rest, — you snatched me from a watery grave. I thank you for your goodness, — though I am sorry you saved my life. The world is full of forsaken women. I did not wish to add another to the number."

Sophie then fell silent and began weeping afresh. My good master took her hand with the greatest delicacy.

"My child," he said, "I have listened with a tender interest to the story of your life, and I own 't is a sad tale. But I am happy to discern that your case is curable. Not only was your lover unworthy of the favours you showed him and has proved himself on trial a selfish, cruel-hearted libertine, but I see plainly your love for him was only an impulse of the senses and the effect of your own sensibility, the particular object of which mattered far less than you imagine. What there was rare and excellent in the liaison came from you. Well then, nothing is lost, since the source still remains. Your eyes, which have thrown a glamour of the fairest hues over, I doubt not, a very ordinary individual, will not cease to go on shedding abroad elsewhere the same bright rays of charming self-delusion."

My good master said more in the same strain, dropping from his lips the finest words ever heard anent the tribulations of the senses and the errors lovers are prone to. But, as he talked on, Sophie, who for some while had let her pretty head droop on the shoulder of this best of men, fell softly asleep. When M. l'Abbé Coignard saw his young friend was wrapped in a sound slumber, he congratulated himself on having discoursed in a vein so meet to afford repose and peace to a suffering soul.

"It must be allowed," he chuckled, "my sermons have a beneficent effect."

Not to disturb Mademoiselle's slumbers, he took a thousand pretty precautions, amongst others constraining himself to talk on uninterruptedly, not unreasonably apprehensive that a sudden silence might awake her.

"Tournebroche, my son," he said, turning

to me, "look, all her sorrows are vanished away with the consciousness she had of them. You must see they were all of the imagination and resided in her own thought. You must understand likewise they sprang from a certain pride and overweening conceit that goes along with love and makes it very exacting. For, in truth, if only we loved in humbleness of spirit and forgetfulness of self, or merely with a simple heart, we should be content with what is vouchsafed us and should not straightway cry treason when some slight is put on us. And if some power of loving were left us still, after our lover had deserted us, we should await the issue in calmness of mind to make what use of it God should please to grant."

But the day was just breaking by this time, and the song of the birds grew so loud it drowned my good master's voice. He made no complaint on this score.

"Hearken," he said, "to the sparrows. They make love more wisely than men do."

Sophie awoke in the white light of dawn, and I admired her lovely eyes, which fatigue and grief had ringed with a delicate pearly grey. She seemed somewhat reconciled to life, and did not refuse a cup of chocolate which my good master made her drink at Mathurine's door, the pretty chocolate-seller of the Halles.

But as the poor child came into more complete possession of her wits, she began to trouble about sundry practical difficulties she had not thought of till then.

"What will my aunt say? And whatever can I tell her?" she asked distractedly.

The aunt lived just opposite Saint-Eustache, less than a hundred yards from Mathurine's archway. Thither we escorted her niece; and M. l'Abbé Coignard, who had quite a venerable look, though one shoe *was* unbuckled, accompanied the fair Sophie to the door of her aunt's lodging and pitched that lady a fine tale:

"I had the happy fortune," he informed her, "to encounter your good niece at the very moment when she was assailed by four footpads armed with pistols, and I shouted for the watch so lustily that the thieves took to their heels in a panic. But they were not quick enough to escape the sergeants who, by the rarest chance, ran up in answer to my outcries. They arrested the villains after a desperate tussle. I took my share of the rough and tumble, and I thought at first I had lost my hat in the fray. When all was over, we were all taken, your niece, the four footpads and myself, before his Honour the Lieutenant-Criminel, who treated us with much consideration and detained us till daylight in his cabinet, taking down our evidence."

The aunt answered drily:

"I thank you, sir, for having saved my niece from a peril which, to say the truth, is not the risk a girl of her age need fear the most, when she is out alone at night in the streets of Paris."

My good master made no answer to this; but Mademoiselle Sophie spoke up and said in a voice of deep feeling:

"I do assure you, Aunt, Monsieur l'Abbé saved my life."

. . . .

Some years after this singular adventure, my master made the fatal journey to Lyons from which he never returned. He was foully murdered, and I had the ineffable grief of seeing him expire in my arms. The incidents of his death have no connexion with the matter I speak of here. I have taken pains to record them elsewhere; they are indeed memorable, and will never, I think, be forgotten. I may add that this journey was in all ways unfortunate, for after losing the best of masters on the road, I was likewise forsaken by a mistress who loved me, but did not love me alone, and whose loss nearly broke my heart, coming after that of my good master. It is a mistake to suppose that a man who has received one cruel blow grows callous to succeeding strokes of calamity. Far otherwise; he suffers agonies from the smallest contrarieties. I returned to Paris in a state of dejection almost beyond belief.

Well, one evening, by way of enlivening my spirits, I went to the Comédie, where they were playing *Bajazet*, one of Racine's excellent pieces. I was particularly struck by the charm and beauty, no less than the originality and talent, of the actress who took the part of Roxane. She expressed with a delightful naturalness the passion animating that character, and I shuddered as I heard her declaim in accents that were harmonious and yet terrible the line:

Écoutez, Bajazet, je sens que je vous aime.*

I never wearied of gazing at her all the time she occupied the stage, and admiring the beauty of her eyes that gleamed below a brow as pure as marble and crowned by powdered locks all spangled with pearls. Her slender waist too, which her hoop showed off to perfection, did not fail to make a vivid impression on my heart. I had the better leisure to scrutinize these adorable charms as she happened to face in my direction to deliver several important portions of her rôle. And the more I looked, the more I felt convinced I had seen her before, though I found it impossible to recall anything connected with our previous meeting. My neighbour in the theatre, who was a constant frequenter of the Comédie, told me the beautiful actress was

* " Hearken, Bajazet, I feel I love you."

Mademoiselle B——, the idol of the pit. He added that she was as great a favourite in society as on the boards, that M. le Duc de La —— had made her the fashion and that she was on the highroad to eclipse Mademoiselle Lecouvreur.

I was just leaving my seat after the performance when a "femme de chambre" handed me a note in which I found written in pencil the words:

"*Mademoiselle Roxane is waiting for you in her coach at the theatre door.*"

I could not believe the missive was intended for me; and I asked the abigail who had delivered it if she was not mistaken in the recipient.

"If I *am* mistaken," she replied confidently, "then you cannot be Monsieur de Tournebroche, that is all."

I ran to the coach which stood waiting in front of the House, and inside I recognized Mademoiselle B——, her head muffled in a black satin hood.

She beckoned to me to get in, and when I was seated beside her:

"Do you not," she asked me, "recognize Sophie, whom you rescued from drowning on the banks of the Seine?"

"What! you! Sophie — Roxane — Mademoiselle B——, is it possible?—"

My confusion was extreme, but she appeared to view it without annoyance.

"I saw you," she went on, "in one corner of the pit. I knew you instantly and played for you. Say, did I play well? I am so glad to see you again!—"

She asked me news of M. l'Abbé Coignard, and when I told her my good master had just perished miserably, she burst into tears.

She was good enough to inform me of the chief events of her life:

"My aunt," she said, "used to mend her laces for Madame de Saint-Remi, who, as you must know, is an admirable actress. A short while after the night when you did me such yeoman service, I went to her house to take home some pieces of lace. The lady told me I had a face that interested her. She then asked me to read some verses, and concluded I was not without wits. She had me trained.

I made my first appearance at the Comédie last year. I interpret passions I have felt myself, and the public credits me with some talent. M. le Duc de La —— exhibits a very dear friendship for me, and I think he will never cause me pain and disappointment, because I have learnt to ask of men only what they can give. At this moment he is expecting me at supper. I must not break my word."

But, reading my vexation in my eyes, she added:

"However, I have told my people to go the longest way round and to drive slowly."

CHILD LIFE IN TOWN AND COUNTRY

FANCHON

I

ANCHON went early one morning, like Little Red Riding-Hood, to see her grandmother, who lives right at the other end of the village. But Fanchon did not stop like little Red Riding-Hood, to gather nuts in the wood. She went straight on her way and she did not meet the wolf.

From a long way off she saw her grandmother sitting on the stone step at her cottage door, a smile on her toothless mouth and her arms, as dry and knotty as an old vine-stock, open to welcome her little granddaughter. It rejoices Fanchon's heart to spend a whole day with her grandmother; and her grandmother, whose trials and troubles are all over and who lives as happy as a cricket in the warm chimney-corner, is rejoiced too to see her son's little girl, the picture of her own childhood.

They have many things to tell each other, for one of them is coming back from the journey of life which the other is setting out on.

"You grow a bigger girl every day," says the old grandmother to Fanchon, "and every day I get smaller; I scarcely need now to stoop at all to touch your forehead. What matters my great age when I can see the roses of my girlhood blooming again in your cheeks, my pretty Fanchon?"

But Fanchon asked to be told again — for the hundredth time — all about the glittering paper flowers under the glass shade, the coloured pictures where our Generals in brilliant uniforms are overthrowing their enemies, the gilt cups, some of which have lost their handles, while others have kept theirs, and grandfather's gun that hangs above the chimney-piece from the nail where he put it up himself for the last time, thirty years ago.

But time flies, and the hour is come to get ready the midday dinner. Fanchon's grandmother stirs up the drowsy fire; then she breaks the eggs on the black earthenware platter. Fanchon is deeply interested in the bacon omelette as she watches it browning and sputtering over the fire. There is no one in the world like her grandmother for making omelettes and telling pretty stories. Fanchon sits on the settle, her chin on a level with the table, to eat the steaming omelette and drink the sparkling cider. But her grandmother eats her dinner, from force of habit, standing at the fireside. She holds her knife in her right hand, and in the other a crust of bread with her toothsome morsel on it. When both have done eating:

"Grandmother," says Fanchon, "tell me the 'Blue Bird.'"

And her grandmother tells Fanchon how, by the spite of a bad fairy, a beautiful Prince was changed into a sky-blue bird, and of the grief the Princess felt when she heard of the transformation and saw her love fly all bleeding to the window of the Tower where she was shut up.

Fanchon thinks and thinks.

"Grandmother," she says at last, "is it a

great while ago the Blue Bird flew to the Tower where the Princess was shut up?"

Her grandmother tells her it was many a long day since, in the times when the animals used to talk.

"You were young then?" asks Fanchon.

"I was not yet born," the old woman tells her.

And Fanchon says:

"So, grandmother, there were things in the world even before you were born?"

And when their talk is done, her grandmother gives Fanchon an apple with a hunch of bread and bids her:

"Run away, little one; go and play and eat your apple in the garden."

And Fanchon goes into the garden, where there are trees and grass and flowers and birds.

II

ER grandmother's garden was full of grass and flowers and trees, and Fanchon thought it was the prettiest garden in all the world. By this time she had pulled out her pocket-knife to cut her bread with, as they do in the village. First she munched her apple, then she began upon her bread. Presently a little bird came fluttering past her. Then a second came, and a third. Soon ten, twenty, thirty were crowding round Fanchon. There were grey birds, and red, there were yellow birds, and green, and blue. And all were pretty and they all sang. At first Fanchon could not think what they wanted. But she soon saw they were asking for bread and that they were little beggars. Yes, they were beggars, but they were singers as well. Fanchon was too kind-hearted to refuse bread to any one who paid for it with songs.

She was a little country girl, and she did not know that once long ago, in a country where white cliffs of marble are washed by the blue sea, a blind old man earned his daily bread by singing the shepherds' songs which the learned still admire to-day. But her heart laughed to hear the little birds, and she tossed them crumbs that never reached the ground, for the birds always caught them in the air.

Fanchon saw that the birds were not all the same in character. Some would stand in a ring round her feet waiting for the crumbs to fall into their beaks. These were philosophers. Others again she could see circling nimbly on the wing all about her. She even noticed one little thief that darted in and pecked shamelessly at her own slice.

She broke the bread and threw crumbs to them all; but all could not get some to eat. Fanchon found that the boldest and cleverest left nothing for the others.

"That is not fair," she told them; "each of you ought to take his proper turn."

But they never heeded; nobody ever does, when you talk of fairness and justice. She tried every way to favour the weak and hearten the timid; but she could make nothing of it, and do what she would, she fed the big fat birds at the expense of the thin ones. This made her sorry; she was such a simple child she did not know it is the way of the world.

Crumb by crumb, the bread all went down the little singers' throats. And Fanchon went back very happy to her grandmother's house.

III

WHEN night fell, her grandmother took the basket in which Fanchon had brought her a cake, filled it with apples and grapes, hung it on the child's arm, and said:

"Now, Fanchon, go straight back home, without stopping to play with the village ragamuffins. Be a good girl always. Good-bye."

Then she kissed her. But Fanchon stood thinking at the door.

"Grandmother?" she said.

"What is it, little Fanchon?"

"I should like to know," said Fanchon, "if there are any beautiful Princes among the birds that ate up my bread."

"Now that there are no more fairies," her grandmother told her, "the birds are all birds and nothing else."

"Good-bye, grandmother."

"Good-bye, Fanchon."

And Fanchon set off across the meadows for her home, the chimneys of which she could see smoking a long way off against the red sky of sunset.

On the road she met Antoine, the gardener's little boy. He asked her:

"Will you come and play with me, Fanchon?"

But she answered:

"I won't stop to play with you, because my grandmother told me not to. But I will give you an apple, because I love you very much."

Antoine took the apple and kissed the little girl.

They loved each other fondly.

He called her his little wife, and she called him her little husband.

As she went on her way, stepping soberly along like a staid, grown-up person, she heard behind her a merry twittering of birds, and turning round to look, she saw they were the same little pensioners she had fed when they were hungry. They came flying after her.

"Good night, little friends," she called to them, "good night! It's bedtime now, so good night!"

And the winged songsters answered her with little cries that mean "God keep you!" in bird language.

So Fanchon came back to her mother's to the sound of sweet music in the air.

IV

FANCHON lay down in the dark in her little bed, which a carpenter in the village had made long ago of walnut-wood and carved a light railing alongside. The good old man had been resting years and years now under the shadow of the church, in a grass-grown bed; for Fanchon's cot had been her grandfather's when he was a little lad, and he had slept where she sleeps now. A curtain of pink-sprigged cotton protects her slumbers; she sleeps, and in her dreams she sees the Blue Bird flying to his sweetheart's Castle. She thinks he is as beautiful as a star, but she never expects him to come and light on her shoulder. She knows *she* is not a Princess, and no Prince changed into a blue bird will come to visit her. She tells herself that all birds are not Princes; that the birds of her village are villagers, and that there might be one perhaps found amongst them, a little country lad changed into a sparrow by a bad fairy and wearing in his heart under his brown feathers the love of little Fanchon. Yes, if *he* came and she knew him, she would give him not bread crumbs only, but cake and kisses. She would so like to see him, and lo! she sees him; he comes and perches on her shoulder. He is a jack-sparrow, only a common sparrow. He has nothing rich or rare about him, but he looks alert and lively. To tell the truth, he is a little torn and tattered; he lacks a feather in his tail; he has lost it in battle — unless it was through some bad fairy of the village. Fanchon has her suspicions he is a naughty bird. But she is a girl, and she does not mind her jack-sparrow being a trifle headstrong, if only he has a kind heart. She pets him and calls him pretty names. Suddenly he begins to grow bigger; his body gets longer; his wings turn into two arms; he is a boy, and Fanchon knows who he is — Antoine, the gardener's little lad, who asks her:

"Shall we go and play together, shall we, Fanchon?"

She claps her hands for joy, and away she goes. . . . But suddenly she wakes and rubs her eyes. Her sparrow is gone, and so is Antoine! She is all alone in her little room. The dawn, peeping in between the flowered curtains, throws a white, innocent light over her cot. She can hear the birds singing in the garden. She jumps out of bed in her little nightgown and opens the window; she looks out into the garden, which is gay with flowers — roses, geraniums, and convolvulus — and spies her little pensioners, her little musicians, of yesterday. There they all sit in a row on the garden-fence, singing her a morning hymn to pay her for their crumbs of bread.

THE FANCY-DRESS BALL

HERE we have little boys who are conquering heroes and little girls who are heroines. Here we have shepherdesses in hoops and wreaths of roses and shepherds in satin coats, who carry crooks tied with knots of riband. Oh! what white, pretty sheep they must be these shepherds tend! Here are Alexander the Great and Zaïre, and Pyrrhus and Merope, Mahomet, Harlequin, Pierrot, Scapin, Blaise and Babette. They have come from all parts, from Greece and Rome and the lands of Faëry, to dance together. What a fine thing a fancy ball is, and how delicious to be a great King for an hour or a famous Princess! There is nothing to spoil the pleasure. No need to act up to your costume, nor even to talk in character.

THE FANCY-DRESS BALL

It would be poor fun, mind you, to wear heroes' clothes if you had to have a hero's heart as well. Heroes' hearts are torn with all sorts of sorrows. They are most of them famous for their calamities. If they had lived happy, we should never have heard of them. Merope had no wish to dance. Pyrrhus was cruelly slain by Orestes just when he was going to wed, and the innocent Zaïre perished by the hand of her lover the Turk, philosophical Turk though he was. As for Blaise and Babette, the song says they suffer fond regrets that go on forever.

Why speak of Pierrot and Scapin? You know as well as I do they were scamps, and got their ears pulled more than once. No! glory costs too dear, even Harlequin's. On the contrary, it is very agreeable to be little boys and girls, and have the look of being great personages. That is why there is no pleasure to compare with a fancy ball, when the dresses are splendid enough. Only to wear them makes you feel brave. Then think how proud and pretty all your little friends are with their feathers and mantles;

how gallant and gay and noble they look, and how like the fine folks of olden times.

In the gallery, where you cannot see them, the musicians, with sad, gentle faces, are tuning up their fiddles. A stately quadrille lies open on their stands. They are going to attack the old-fashioned piece. At the first notes our heroes and masks will lead off the dance.

THE SCHOOL

I PROCLAIM Mademoiselle Genseigne's school the best girls' school in the world. I declare miscreants and slanderers any who shall think or say the contrary. Mademoiselle Genseigne's pupils are all well-behaved and industrious, and there is no pleasanter sight to see than all their small figures sitting so still, and all the heads in a straight row. They look like so many little bottles into which Mademoiselle Genseigne is busy pouring useful knowledge.

Mademoiselle Genseigne sits very upright at her high desk. She has a gentle, serious face; her neatly braided hair and her black tippet inspire respect and sympathy.

Mademoiselle Genseigne, who is very clever, is teaching her little pupils cyphering. She says to Rose Benoît:

"Rose Benoît, if I take four from twelve, what have I left?"

"Four?" answers Rose Benoît.

Mademoiselle Genseigne is not satisfied with the answer.

"And you, Emmeline Capel, if I take four from twelve, how much have I left?"

"Eight," Emmeline Capel answers.

"You hear, Rose Benoît, I have eight left," insists Mademoiselle Genseigne.

Rose Benoît falls into a brown study. Mademoiselle Genseigne has eight left, she is told, but she has no notion if it is eight hats or eight handkerchiefs, or possibly eight apples or eight feathers. The doubt has long tormented her. She can make nothing of arithmetic.

On the other hand, she is very wise in Scripture History. Mademoiselle Genseigne has not another pupil who can describe the Garden of Eden or Noah's Ark as Rose Benoît can. Rose Benoît knows every flower in the Garden and all the animals in the Ark. She knows as many fairy tales as Mademoiselle Genseigne herself. She knows

THE SCHOOL

all the fables of the Fox and the Crow, the Donkey and the Little Dog, the Cock and the Hen, and what they said to each other. She is not at all surprised to hear that the animals used once to talk. The wonder would be if some one told her they don't talk now. She is quite sure she understands what her big dog Tom says and her little canary Chirp. She is quite right; animals have always talked, and they talk still; but they only talk to their friends. Rose Benoît loves them and they love her, and that is why she understands what they say. To understand each other there is nothing like loving one another.

To-day Rose Benoît has said her lessons without a mistake. She has won a good mark. Emmeline Capel has a good mark, too, for knowing her arithmetic lesson so well.

On coming out of school, she told her mother she had a good mark. Then she asked her:

"A good mark, mother, what's the use of it?"

"A good mark is of no use," Emmeline's mother answered; "that is the very reason why we should be proud to get one. You will find out one day, my child, that the rewards most highly esteemed are just those that bring honour without profit."

MARIE

ITTLE girls long to pluck flowers and stars — it is their nature to. But stars will not be plucked, and the lesson they teach little girls is, that in this world there are longings that are never satisfied. Mademoiselle Marie has gone into the park, where she came upon a bed of hydrangeas; she saw how pretty the flowers were and that made her gather one. It was very difficult; she dragged with both hands, and very nearly tumbled over backwards when the stalk broke. She is pleased and proud at what she has done. But nurse has seen her. She runs up, snatches at Mademoiselle Marie's arm, scolds her, and sets her to stand and repent, not in the black closet, but at the foot of a great chestnut, under the shade of a huge Japanese umbrella.

There Mademoiselle Marie sits and thinks, in great surprise and perplexity. Her flower in one hand and the umbrella making a bright halo round her, she looks like a little idol from overseas.

Nurse has told her: "Marie, you must not put that flower in your mouth. If you do it when I tell you not, your little dog Toto will come and eat up your ears." And with these terrible words she walks away.

The young culprit, sitting quite still under her brilliant canopy, looks about her and gazes at earth and sky. It is a big world she sees, big enough and beautiful enough to amuse a little girl for some while. But her hydrangea blossom is more interesting than all the rest put together. She thinks to herself: "It is a flower; it must smell good?" And she puts her nose to the pretty pink and blue ball; she sniffs, but she cannot smell anything. She is not very good at scenting perfume; it is only a short while since she always used to blow at a rose instead of inhaling its odour. You must not laugh at her for that; one cannot learn everything at once.

Besides, if she had as keen a sense of smell as her mother, she would be no better off in this case. A hydrangea *has* no scent; that is why we get tired of it, for all its loveliness. But now Mademoiselle Marie begins to think: "Perhaps it's made of sugar, this flower." Then she opens her mouth very wide and is just going to lift the flower to her lips.

But suddenly, *yap!* goes her little dog. It is Toto, who comes bounding over a geranium bed and comes to a stand right in front of Mademoiselle Marie, with his ears cocked straight up, and stares hard at her out of his sharp little round eyes.

THE PANDEAN PIPES

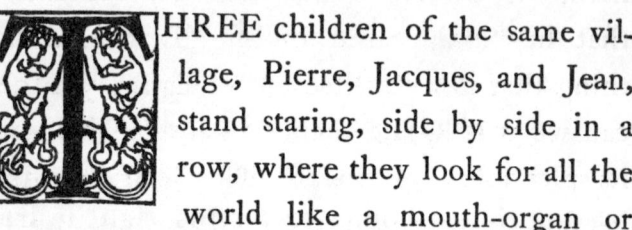THREE children of the same village, Pierre, Jacques, and Jean, stand staring, side by side in a row, where they look for all the world like a mouth-organ or Pandean Pipes, only with three pipes instead of seven. Pierre, to the left, is a tall lad; Jean, to the right, is a short child; Jacques, who is betwixt the two, may call himself tall *or* short, according as he looks at his left-hand or his right-hand neighbour. It is a situation I would beg you to ponder, for it is your own, and mine, and everybody else's. Each one of us is just like Jacques, and deems himself great or small according as his neighbours' inches are many or few.

That is the reason why it is true to say that Jacques is neither tall nor short, and why it is also true to say he is tall *and* he is short. He

THE PANDEAN PIPES

is what God chooses him to be. For us, he is the middle reed of our living Pandean Pipes.

But what is he doing, and what are his two comrades doing? They are staring, staring hard, all three. What at? At something that has disappeared in the distance, something that has vanished out of sight; yet they can see it still, and their eyes are dazzled with its splendours. It makes little Jean clean forget his eel-skin whiplash and the peg-top he has always been so fond of keeping for ever spinning with it in the dusty roads. Pierre and Jacques stand stolidly, their hands behind their backs.

What is the wonderful sight that has bewildered all three? A pedlar's cart, a handcart; they had seen it stop in the village street.

Then the pedlar drew back his oil-cloth covering, and all, men, women, and children, feasted their eyes on knives, scissors, popguns, jumping Jacks, wooden soldiers and lead soldiers, bottles of scent, cakes of soap, coloured pictures, and a thousand other splendid objects. The servant-wenches from the farm and the mill turned pale with longing; Pierre and Jacques flushed red with delight. Little Jean put out his tongue at it all. Everything the barrow held seemed to them rich and rare. But what they coveted most of all were those myterious articles whose meaning and use they could make nothing of. For instance, there were polished globes like mirrors that reflected their faces with the features ludicrously distorted. There were Epinal wares with figures in impossibly vivid colours; there were little cases and boxes with nobody knows what inside.

The women made purchases of muslins and laces by the yard, and the pedlar rolled the black oil-cloth cover back again over the treasures of his barrow. Then, pulling at the collar, he hauled off his load after him along the highroad. And now barrow and barrow-man have disappeared below the horizon.

ROGER'S STUD

IT is a great anxiety keeping a stud. The horse is a delicate animal and needs a lot of looking after. Just ask Roger if it does n't!

He is busy now grooming his noble chestnut, which would be the pearl of wooden horses, the flower of the Black Forest studfarms, if only he had not lost half his tail in battle. Roger would so like to know whether wooden horses' tails grow again.

After rubbing them down in fancy, Roger gives his horses an imaginary feed of oats. That is the proper way to feed these elfin creatures of wood on whose backs little boys gallop through the land of dreams.

Now Roger is off for his ride, mounted on his mettled charger. The poor beast has no ears left and his mane is all notched like an old broken comb; but Roger loves him. Why it would be hard to say! This bay was the gift of a poor man; and the presents of the poor are somehow sweeter perhaps than any others.

Roger is off. He has ridden far. The flowers of the carpet are the blossoms of the tropical forest. Good luck to you, little Roger! May your hobby-horse carry you happily through the world! May you never have a more dangerous mount! Small and great, we all ride ours! Which of us has not his hobby?

Men's hobbies gallop like mad things along the roads of life; one is chasing glory, another pleasure; many leap over precipices and break their rider's neck. I wish you luck, little Roger, and I hope, when you are a man, you will bestride two hobbies that will always carry you along the right road; one is spirited, the other gentle-tempered; they are both noble steeds; one is called Courage and the other Kindness.

COURAGE

LOUISON and Frédéric are off to school along the village street. The sun shines gaily and the two children are singing. They sing like the nightingale, because their hearts are light like his. They sing an old song their grandmothers sang when they were little girls, a song their children's children will sing one day; for songs are tender flowers that never die, they fly from lip to lip down the ages. The lips fade and fall silent one after the other, but the song lives on for ever. There are songs come down to us from the days when the men were shepherds and all the women shepherdesses. That is the reason why they speak of nothing but sheep and wolves.

Louison and Frédéric sing; their mouths are as round as a flower and the song rises shrill and thin and clear in the morning air.

But listen! suddenly the notes stick in Frédéric's throat.

What unseen power is it has strangled the music on the boy's lips? It is fear. Every day, as sure as fate, he comes upon the butcher's dog at the end of the village street, and every day his heart seems to stop and his legs begin to shake at the sight. Yet the butcher's dog does not fly at him, or even threaten to. He sits peaceably at his master's shop-door. But he is black, and he has a staring bloodshot eye and shows a row of sharp white teeth. He looks frightful. And then he squats there in the middle of bits of meat and offal and all sorts of horrors — which makes him more terrifying still. Of course it is n't his fault, but he is the presiding genius. Yes, a savage brute, the butcher's dog! So, the instant Frédéric catches sight of the beast before the shop, he picks up a big stone, as he sees grown-up men do to keep off bad-tempered curs, and he slinks past close, close under the opposite wall.

That is how he behaved this time; and Louison laughed at him.

She did not make any of those daredevil speeches one generally caps with others more reckless still. No, she never said a word; she never stopped singing. But she altered her voice and began singing on such a mocking note that Frédéric reddened to his very ears. Then his little head began to buzz with many thoughts. He learned that we must dread shame even more than danger. And he was afraid of being afraid.

So, when school was over and he saw the butcher's dog, he marched undauntedly past the astonished animal.

History adds that he kept a corner of his eye on Louison to see if she was looking. It is a true saying that, if there were no dames nor damsels in the world, men would be less courageous.

CATHERINE'S "AT HOME"

IT is five o'clock. Mademoiselle Catherine is "at home" to her dolls. It is her "day." The dolls do not talk; the little Genie that gave them their smile did not vouchsafe the gift of speech. He refused it for the general good; if dolls could talk, we should hear nobody but them. Still there is no lack of conversation. Mademoiselle Catherine talks for her guests as well as for herself; she asks questions and gives the answers.

"How do you do? — Very well, thank you. I broke my arm yesterday morning going to buy cakes. But it's quite well now. — Ah! so much the better. — And how is your little girl? — She has the whooping-cough. — Ah! what a pity! Does she cough much? — Oh! no, it's a whooping-cough where there's no cough. You know I had two more children last week. — Really? that makes four doesn't it? — Four or five, I've forgotten which. When you have so many, you get confused. — What a pretty frock you have. — Oh! I've got far prettier ones still at home. — Do you go to the theatre? — Yes, every evening. I was at the Opera yesterday; but Polichinelle wasn't playing, because the wolf had eaten him. — I go to dances every day, my dear. — It is so amusing. — Yes, I wear a blue gown and dance with the young men, Generals, Princes, Confectioners, all the most distinguished people. — You look as pretty as an angel to-day, my dear. — Oh! it's the spring. — Yes, but what a pity it's snowing. — *I* love the snow, because it's white. — Oh! there's black snow, you know. — Yes, but that's the bad snow."

There's fine conversation for you; Mademoiselle Catherine's tongue goes nineteen to the dozen. Still I have one fault to find with her; she talks all the time to the same visitor, who is pretty and wears a fine frock.

There she is wrong. A good hostess is equally gracious to all her guests. She treats them all with affability, and if she shows any particular preference, it is to the more retiring and the less prosperous. We should flatter the unhappy; it is the only flattery allowable. But Catherine has discovered this for herself. She has guessed the secret of true politeness: a kind heart is everything. She pours out tea for the company, and forgets nobody. On the contrary, she presses the dolls that are poor and unhappy and shy to help themselves to invisible cakes and sandwiches made of dominoes.

Some day Catherine will hold a salon where the old French courtesy will live again.

LITTLE SEA-DOGS

THEY are sailor boys, regular little sea-dogs. Look at them; they have their caps pulled down over their ears so that the gale blowing in from the sea and bringing the spindrift with it may not deafen them with its dreadful howling. They wear heavy woollen clothes to keep out the cold and wet. Their patched pea-jacket and breeches have been their elders' before them. Most of their garments have been contrived out of old things of their father's. Their soul is likewise of the same stuff as their father's; it is simple, brave, and long-suffering. At birth they inherited a single-hearted, noble temper. Who and what gave it them? After God and their parents, the Sea. The Sea teaches sailors courage by teaching them to face danger. It is a rough but kindly instructor.

That is why our little sailor-boys, though their hearts are childlike still, have the spirit of gallant veterans. Elbows on the parapet of the sea-wall, they gaze out into the offing. It is more than the blue line marking the faint division between sea and sky that they see. Their eyes care little for the soft, changing colours of the ocean or the vast, contorted masses of the clouds. What they see, as they look seawards, is something more moving than the hue of the waves or the shape of the clouds; it is a suggestion of human love. They are spying for the boats that sailed away for the fishing; presently they will loom again on the horizon, laden with shrimp to the gunwales, and bringing home uncles and big brothers and fathers. The little fleet will soon appear yonder betwixt the ocean and God's sky with its white or brown sails. To-day the sky is unclouded, the sea calm; the flood tide floats the fishers gently to the shore. But the Ocean is a capricious old fellow, who takes all shapes and sings in many voices. To-day he laughs; to-morrow he will be growling in the night under his beard of foam. He shipwrecks the most handy boats, though they have been blessed by the Priest to the chanting of the *Te Deum;* he drowns the most skilful master mariners, and it is all his fault you see in the village, before the cottage doors where the nets hang to dry beside the fish-creels, so many women wearing black widow's weeds.

GETTING WELL

ERMAINE is ill. Nobody knows how it began. The arm which shows fever is invisible like the dustman's hand, the old fellow who comes every night and makes the little ones so sleepy. But Germaine was not ill very long and she was not very bad, and now she is getting well again. This getting well is even pleasanter than being quite well, which comes next. In the same way hoping and wishing are better, very often, than anything we wish for or hope for. Germaine lies in bed in her pretty, bright room, and her dreams are as bright-coloured as her room.

She looks, a little languidly still, at her doll, which sleeps beside her own bed. There are sympathies that go deep between little girls and their dolls. Germaine's doll

GETTING WELL

fell ill at the same time as her little mamma, and now she is getting well with her. She will take her first carriage outing sitting by Germaine's side.

She has seen the doctor too. Alfred came to feel the doll's pulse. He is Doctor "As-bad-as-can-be." He talks of nothing but cutting off arms and legs. But Germaine asked him so earnestly that he agreed to cure her dolly without slashing it to pieces. But he prescribed the nastiest medicines.

Illness has one advantage at any rate; it makes us know our friends. Germaine is sure now she can count on Alfred's goodness; she is certain Lucie is the best of sisters. All the nine days her illness lasted, Lucie came to learn her lessons and do her sewing in the sick room. She insists on bringing the little patient her herb-tea herself. And it is not a bitter potion, such as Alfred ordered; no, it is balmy with the scent of wild flowers.

When she smells its perfume, Germaine's thoughts fly to the flowery mountain paths, the haunt of children and bees, where she played so often last year. Alfred too remembers the beautiful ways, and the woods, and the springs, and the mules that climbed up and up on the brink of precipices with a sound of tinkling bells.

ACROSS THE MEADOWS

AFTER breakfast Catherine started off to the meadows with her little brother Jean. When they set out, the day seemed as young and fresh as they were. The sky was not altogether blue; it was grey rather, but of a tenderer grey than any blue. Catherine's eyes are just the same grey, as if made out of a bit of morning sky.

Catherine and Jean wander all by themselves through the fields. Their mother is a farmer's wife and is at work at home. They have no nurse-maid to take them, and they don't need one. They know their way, and all the woods and fields and hills. Catherine can tell the time by looking at the sun, and she has guessed all sorts of pretty secrets of Nature that town-bred children have no suspicion of. Little Jean himself understands a great many things about the woods, the pools, and the mountains, for his little soul is a country soul.

Catherine and Jean go roaming through the flowery meadows. As they go, Catherine gathers a nosegay. She picks blue centauries, scarlet poppies, cuckoo-flowers, and buttercups, which she also knows as *little chicks*. She picks those pretty purple blossoms that grow in hedgerows and are called Venus' looking-glasses. She picks the dark ears of the milkwort, and crane's-bill and lily of the valley, whose tiny white bells shed a delicious perfume at the least puff of wind. Catherine loves flowers because they are beautiful; and she loves them too because they make such pretty ornaments. She is very simply dressed, and her pretty hair is hid under a brown linen cap. She wears a cotton check pinafore over her plain frock, and goes in wooden shoes. She has never seen rich dresses except on the Virgin Mary and the St. Catherine in the parish church. But there are some things little girls know directly they are born. Catherine knows that flowers are becoming to wear, and that pretty ladies who pin nosegays in their bosoms look lovelier than ever. So she has a notion she must be very fine indeed now, carrying a nosegay bigger than her own head. Her thoughts are as bright and fragrant as her flowers. They are thoughts that cannot be put into words; there are no words pretty enough. It wants song tunes for that, the liveliest and softest airs, the sweetest songs. So Catherine sings, as she gathers her nosegay: "Away to the woods alone" and "My heart is for him, my heart is for him."

Little Jean is of another temper. He follows another line of ideas. He is a broth of a boy, he is; Jean is not breeched yet, but his spirit is beyond his years and there's no more rollicking blade than he. While he grips his sister's pinafore with one hand, for fear of tumbling, he shakes his whip in the other like a sturdy lad. His father's head stableman can hardly crack his any better when he meets his sweetheart, bringing home the horses from watering at the river. Little Jean is lulled by no soft reveries. He never heeds the field flowers. The games he dreams of are stiff jobs of work. His thoughts dwell on wagons stogged in the mire and big cart-horses hauling at the collar at his voice and under his lash.

Catherine and Jean have climbed above the meadows, up the hill, to a high ground from which you can make out all the chimneys of the village dotted among the trees and in the far distance the steeples of six parishes. Then you see what a big place the world is. Then Catherine can better understand the stories she has been taught, — the dove from the Ark, the Israelites in the Promised Land, and Jesus going from city to city.

"Let's sit down there," she says.

Down she sits, and, opening her hands, she sheds her flowery harvest all over her. She is all fragrant with blossoms, and in a moment the butterflies come fluttering round her. She picks and chooses and matches her flowers; she weaves them into garlands and wreaths, and hangs flower-bells in her ears; she is decked out now like the rustic image of a Holy Virgin the shepherds venerate. Her little brother Jean, who has been busy all this while driving a team of imaginary horses, sees her in all this bravery. Instantly he is filled with admiration. A religious awe penetrates all his childish soul. He stops, and the whip falls from his fingers. He feels that she is beautiful and all smothered in lovely flowers. He tries in vain to say all this in his soft, indistinct speech. But she has guessed. Little Catherine is his big sister, and a big sister is a little mother; she foresees, she guesses; she has the sacred instinct.

"Yes, darling," cries Catherine, "I am going to make you a beautiful wreath, and you will look like a little king."

And so she twines together the white flowers, the yellow flowers, and the red flowers, into a chaplet. She puts it on little Jean's head, and he flushes with pride and pleasure. She kisses her little brother, lifts him in her arms and plants him, all garlanded with blossoms, on a big stone. Then she looks at him admiringly, because he is beautiful and *she* has made him so.

And standing there on his rustic pedestal, little Jean knows he is beautiful, and the thought fills him with a deep respect for himself. He feels he is something holy. Very upright and still, with round eyes and tight-drawn lips, arms by his side with the palms open and the fingers parted like the spokes of a wheel, he tastes a pious joy to be an idol — he is sure he is an idol now. The sky is overhead, the woods and fields lie at his feet. He is the hub of the universe. He alone is great, he alone is beautiful.

But suddenly Catherine breaks into a laugh. She shouts:

"Oh! how funny you look, little Jean! how funny you do look!"

She runs up and throws her arms round him, she kisses him and shakes him; the heavy wreath of flowers slips down over his nose. And she laughs again:

"Oh! how funny he looks! how very funny!"

But it is no laughing matter for little Jean. He is sad and sorry, wondering why it is all over and he has left off being beautiful. It hurts to come down to earth again!

Now the wreath is unwound and tossed on the grass, and little Jean is like anybody else once more. Yes, he has left off being beautiful. But he is still a sturdy young scamp. He soon has his whip in hand again and now he is hauling his team of six, the six big cart-horses of his dreams, out of that rut. Catherine is still playing with her flowers. But some of them are dying. Others are closing in sleep. For the flowers go to sleep like the animals, and look! the campanulas, plucked a few hours ago, are shutting their purple bells and sinking asleep in the little hands that have parted them from life.

A light breeze blows by, and Catherine shivers. It is night coming.

"I am hungry," says little Jean.

But Catherine has not a bit of bread to give her little brother. She says:

"Little brother, let's go back to the house."

And they both think of the cabbage soup steaming in the pot that hangs from the hook right under the great chimney. Catherine gathers her flowers in her arm and taking her little brother by the hand, she leads him homewards.

The sun sank slowly down to the ruddy West. The swallows swooped past the two children, almost touching them with their wings, that hardly seemed to move. It was getting dark. Catherine and Jean pressed closer together.

Catherine dropped her flowers one after the other by the way. They could hear, in the wide silence, the untiring chirp-chirp of the crickets. They were afraid, both of them, and they were sad; the melancholy of nightfall had entered into their little hearts. All round them was familiar ground, but the things they knew the best looked strange and uncanny. The earth seemed suddenly to have grown too big and too old for them. They were tired, and they began to think they would never reach the house, where mother was making the soup for all the family. Jean's whip hung limp and still, and Catherine let the last of her flowers slip from her tired fingers. She was dragging Jean along by the arm, and neither said a word.

At last they saw a long way off the roof of their house and smoke rising in the darkening sky. Then they stopped running, and clapping their hands together, shouted for joy. Catherine kissed her little brother; then they set off running again as fast as ever their weary legs would carry them. When they reached the village, there were women coming back from the fields who gave them good evening. They breathed again. Their mother was on the door-step, in a white cap, soup-ladle in hand.

"Come along, little ones, come along!" she called to them. And they threw themselves into her arms. When she reached the parlour where the cabbage soup was smoking on the table, Catherine shivered again. She had seen night come down over the earth. Jean, seated on the settle, his chin on a level with the table, was already eating his soup.

THE MARCH PAST

ENÉ, Bernard, Roger, Jacques, and Étienne feel sure there is nothing finer in the world than to be a soldier. Francine agrees with them and she would love to be a boy to join the army. They think so because soldiers wear fine uniforms, epaulettes and gold lace, and glittering swords. There is yet another reason for putting the soldier in the front rank of citizens — because he gives his life for his Country. There is no true greatness in this world but that of sacrifice, and to offer one's life is the greatest of all sacrifices, because it includes all others. That is why the hearts of the crowd beat high when a regiment goes by.

René is the General. He wears a cocked hat and rides a war-horse. The hat is made of paper and the horse is a chair. His army

THE MARCH PAST

consists of a drummer and four men — of whom one is a girl! "Shoulder arms! Forward, march!" and the march past begins. Francine and Roger look quite imposing under arms. True, Jacques does not hold his gun very valiantly. He is a melancholy lad. But we must not blame him for that; dreamers can be just as brave as those who never dream at all. His little brother Étienne, the tiniest mite in the regiment, looks pensive. He is ambitious; he would like to be a general officer right away, and that makes him sad.

"Forward! forward!" René shouts the order. "We are to fall on the Chinese, who are in the dining-room." The Chinese are chairs. When you play at fighting, chairs make first-rate Chinese. They fall — and what better can the Chinese do? When all the chairs are feet in air, René announces: "Soldiers, now we have beaten the Chinese, we will have our rations." The idea is well received on all hands. Yes, soldiers must eat. This time the Commissariat has furnished the best of victuals — buns, maids of honour, coffee cakes and chocolate cakes, red-currant syrup. The army falls to with a will. Only Étienne will eat nothing. He frowns and looks enviously at the sword and cocked hat which the General has left on a chair. He creeps up, snatches them, and slips into the next room. There he stands alone before the glass; he puts on the cocked hat and waves the sword; he is a general, a general without an army, a general all to himself. He tastes the pleasures of ambition — pleasures full of vague forecastings and long, long hopes.

DEAD LEAVES

AUTUMN is here. The wind blowing through the woods whirls about the dead leaves. The chestnuts are stripped bare already and lift their black skeleton arms in the air. And now the beeches and hornbeams are shedding *their* leaves. The birches and aspens are turned to trees of gold, and only the great oak keeps his coronal of green.

The morning is fresh; a keen wind is chasing the clouds across a grey sky and reddening the youngsters' fingers. Pierre, Babet, and Jeannot are off to collect the dead leaves, the leaves that once, when they were still alive, were full of dew and songs of birds, and which now strew the ground in thousands and thousands with their little shrivelled corpses. They are dead, but they smell good. They will make a fine litter for Riquette, the goat, and Roussette, the cow. Pierre has taken his big basket; he is quite a little man. Babet has her sack; she is quite a little woman. Jeannot comes last trundling the wheelbarrow.

Down the hill they go at a run. At the edge of the wood they find the other village children, who are come too to lay in a store of dead leaves for the winter. It is not play, this; it is work.

But never think the children are sad, because they are at work. Work is serious, yes; it is not sad. Very often the little ones mimic it in fun, and children's games, most times, are copies of their elders' workaday doings.

Now they are hard at it. The boys do their part in silence. They are peasant lads, and will soon be men, and peasants do not talk much. But it is different with the little peasant girls; *their* tongues go at a fine pace, as they fill the baskets and bags.

But now the sun is climbing higher and warming the country pleasantly. From the cottage roofs rise light puffs of smoke. The

DEAD LEAVES

children know what that means. The smoke tells them the pease-soup is cooking in the pot. One more armful of dead leaves, and the little workers will take the road home. It is a stiff climb. Bending under sacks or toiling behind barrows, they soon get hot, and the sweat comes out in beads. Pierre, Babet and Jeannot stop to take breath.

But the thought of the pease-soup keeps up their courage. Puffing and blowing, they reach home at last. Their mother is waiting for them on the door-step and calls out: "Come along, children, the soup is ready."

Our little friends find this capital. There's no soup so good as what you have worked for.

SUZANNE

THE Louvre, as you know, is a museum where beautiful things and ancient things are kept safe — and this is wisely done, for old age and beauty are both alike venerable. Among the most touching of the antiquities treasured in the Louvre Museum is a fragment of marble, worn and cracked in many places, but on which can still be clearly made out two maidens holding each a flower in her hand. Both are beautiful figures; they were young when Greece was young. They say it was the age of perfect beauty. The sculptor who has left us their image represents them in profile, offering each other one of those lotus flowers that were deemed sacred. In the blue cups of their blossoms the world quaffed oblivion of the ills of life. Our men of learning have given much thought to these two maidens. They have turned over many books to find out about them, big books, bound some in parchment, others in vellum, and many in pig-skin; but they have never fathomed the reason why the two beautiful maidens hold up a flower in their hands.

What they could not discover after so much labour and thought, so many arduous days and sleepless nights, Mademoiselle Suzanne knew in a moment.

Her papa had taken her to the Louvre, where he had business. Mademoiselle Suzanne looked wonderingly at the antiques, and seeing gods with missing arms and legs and heads, she said to herself: "Ah! yes, these are the grown-up gentlemen's dolls; I see now gentlemen break their dollies the same as little girls do." But when she came to the two maidens who, each of them, hold a flower, she threw them a kiss, because they looked so charming. Then her father asked her:

"Why do they give each other a flower?"

And Suzanne answered at once:

"To wish each other a happy birthday."

Then, after thinking a moment, she added:

"They have the same birthday; they are both alike and they are offering each other the same flower. Girl friends should always have the same birthday."

Now Suzanne is far away from the Louvre and the old Greek marbles; she is in the kingdom of the birds and the flowers. She is spending the bright spring days in the meadows under shelter of the woods. She plays in the grass, and that is the sweetest sort of play. She remembers to-day is her little friend Jacqueline's birthday; and so she is going to pick flowers which she will give Jacqueline, and kiss her.

FISHING

JEAN set out betimes in the morning with his sister Jeanne, a fishing-pole over his shoulder and a basket on his arm. It is holiday time and the school is shut; that is why Jean goes off every day with his sister Jeanne, a rod over his shoulder and a basket on his arm, along the river bank. Jean is a Tourainer, and Jeanne a lass of Touraine. The river is Tourainer too. It runs crystal-clear between silvery sallows under a moist, mild sky. Morning and evening white mists trail over the grass of the water-meadows. But Jean and Jeanne love the river neither for the greenery of its banks nor its clear waters that mirror the heavens. They love it for the fish in it. They stop presently at the most likely place, and Jeanne sits down under a pollard willow. Laying down his baskets, Jean unwinds his tackle. This is very primitive — a switch, with a piece of thread and a bent pin at the end of it. Jean supplied the rod, Jeanne gave the line and the hook; so the tackle is the common property of brother and sister. Both want it all to themselves, and this simple contrivance, only meant to do mischief to the fishes, becomes the cause of domestic broils and a rain of blows by the peaceful riverside. Brother and sister fight for the free use of the rod and line. Jean's arm is black and blue with pinches and Jeanne's cheek scarlet from her brother's slaps. At last, when they were tired of pinching and hitting, Jean and Jeanne consented to share amicably what neither could appropriate by force. They agreed that the rod should pass alternately from the brother's hands to the sister's after each fish they caught.

Jean begins. But there's no knowing when he will end. He does not break the treaty openly, but he shirks its consequences by a mean trick. Rather than have to hand over the tackle to his sister, he refuses to catch the

FISHING

fish that come, when they nibble the bait and set his float bobbing.

Jean is artful; Jeanne is patient. She has been waiting six hours. But at last she seems tired of doing nothing. She yawns, stretches, lies down in the shade of the willow, and shuts her eyes. Jean spies her out of one corner of his, and he thinks she is asleep. The float dives. He whips out the line, at the end of which gleams a flash of silver. A gudgeon has taken the pin.

"Ah! it's my turn now," cries a voice behind him.

And Jeanne snatches the rod.

THE PENALTIES OF GREAT-NESS

IT was to go and see their friend Jean that Roger, Marcel, Bernard, Jacques, and Étienne set out along the broad highroad that winds like a handsome yellow riband through the fields and meadows.

Now they are off. They start all abreast; it is the best way. Only there is one defect in the arrangement this time; Étienne is too little to keep up.

He tries hard and puts his best foot foremost. His short legs stretch their widest. He swings his arms into the bargain. But he is too little; he cannot go as fast as his companions. He falls behind because he is too small; it is no use.

The big boys, who are older, should surely wait for him, you say, and suit their pace to

THE PENALTIES OF GREATNESS

his. So they should, but they don't. Forward! cry the strong ones of this world, and they leave the weaklings in the lurch. But hear the end of the story. All of a sudden our four tall, strong, sturdy friends see something jumping on the ground. It jumps because it is a frog, and it wants to reach the meadow along the roadside. The meadow is froggy's home, and he loves it; he has his residence there beside a brook. He jumps, and jumps.

He is a green frog, and he looks like a leaf that is alive. Now the lads are in the meadow; very soon they feel their feet sinking in the soft ground where the rank grass grows. A few steps more, and they are up to their knees in mud. The grass hid a swamp underneath.

They just manage to struggle out. Shoes, socks, calves are all as black as ink. The fairy of the green field has put gaiters of mire on the four bad boys.

Étienne comes up panting for breath. He hardly knows, when he sees them in this pickle, if he should be glad or sorry. His simple little heart is filled with a sense of the catastrophes that befall the great and strong. As for the four muddy urchins, they turn back piteously the way they came, for how can they, I should like to know, how can they go and see their friend Jean with their shoes and stockings in this state? When they get home again, their mothers will know how naughty they have been by the evidence of their legs, while little Étienne's innocence will be legible on his sturdy little stumps.

A CHILD'S DINNER PARTY

HAT fun it is playing at dinner parties! You can have a very plain dinner or a very elaborate one, just as you like. You can manage it with nothing at all. Only you have to pretend a great deal then.

Thérèse and her little sister Pauline have asked Pierre and Marthe to a dinner in the country. Proper invitations have been issued, and they have been talking about it for days. Mamma has given her two little girls good advice — and good things to eat, too. There will be nougat and sweet cakes, and a chocolate cream. The table will be laid in the arbour.

"If only it will be fine!" cries Thérèse, who is nine now. At her age one knows the fondest hopes are often disappointed in this world and you cannot always do what you propose. But little Pauline has none of these worries. She cannot think it will be wet. It will be fine, because she wants it to.

And lo! the great day has broken clear and sunny. Not a cloud in the sky. The two guests have come. How fortunate! For this was another subject of anxiety for Thérèse. Marthe had caught a cold, and perhaps she would not be better in time. As for little Pierre, everybody knows he always misses the train. You cannot blame him for it. It is his misfortune, not his fault. His mother is unpunctual by nature. Everywhere and always little Pierre arrives after everybody else; he has never in his life seen the beginning of anything. This has given him a dull, resigned look.

The dinner is served; ladies and gentlemen, take your places! Thérèse presides. She is thoughtful and serious; the housewifely instinct is awaking in her bosom. Pierre carves valiantly. Nose in the dish and elbows above his head, he struggles to divide the leg of a chicken. Why, his feet even take their part in the tremendous effort. Mademoiselle

A CHILD'S DINNER PARTY

Marthe eats elegantly, without any ado or any noise, just like a grown-up lady. Pauline is not so particular; she eats how she can and as much as she can.

Thérèse, now serving her guests, now one of them herself, is content; and contentment is better than joy. The little dog Gyp has come to eat up the scraps, and Thérèse thinks, as she watches him crunching the bones, that dogs know nothing of all the dainty ways that make grown-up dinners, and children's too, so refined and delightful.

THE ARTIST

MICHEL'S father is a painter. The boy has often watched him at his easel, and seen wonderful pictures of men and animals growing on the canvas, where earth and sea and sky and all nature appear in lifelike colours. He has seen his father lovingly painting women whose eyes and lips seem of flame and dew, women with fair, white skins and smiling mouths. When I am grown up, thinks little Michel, I shall not paint women. I shall paint horses, because that is finer.

Already he tries and tries to draw the finest animals he can imagine. But the horses his fingers make have this about them — they are not a bit like horses. They are more like ostriches on four legs. Yes, painting is very difficult.

THE ARTIST

Still, Michel makes giant strides, and now when you look at his drawings you can make out more or less what they are meant for. He draws every day. He is painstaking and loves the work; and those two things are the best half of genius. Time will do the rest, and perhaps one day Michel will be as great a painter as his father. Yesterday he covered a sheet of foolscap with a fine composition, in which he represented a gentleman, stick in hand, walking by the sea-shore. Except that his arm comes out of his chest, the gentleman is very well drawn. He has four buttons on his coat; what could be more perfect? Near him is a tree. In the distance a boat. The gentleman looks as if he were going to pick up the boat in his hand and wanted to swallow the tree. The perspective is not quite right. They criticise the same fault in the greatest masters.

To-day Michel is finishing a still more ambitious design. It contains men, boats, and windmills. He puts the finishing touch to this great work. He looks at it, and the boats seem to glide over the water and the sails of the windmills to go round. He is proud of himself. He glories in his work, as true artists do, — as God did.

But he has forgotten the kitten playing on the floor beside him with a ball of thread. The moment Michel leaves the room, the little animal will jump up on the table and with a knock of its white paw upset the ink-pot over the papers. Thus will perish Michel's masterpiece. The artist will be down-hearted at first. But soon he will produce another masterpiece to make good the wrong done him by the kitten and cruel fate. So talent rises victorious over ill fortune.

JACQUELINE AND MIRAUT

ACQUELINE and Miraut are old friends. Jacqueline is a little girl, and Miraut is a big dog. They are of the same world, they are both country bred; hence their profound sympathy. How long have they known each other? They cannot tell; it goes beyond a dog's memory and beyond a little girl's. Besides, they don't need to know; they have no wish and no need to know anything. All the idea they have is that they have been friends for a very long time, since the beginning of things; for they cannot conceive, either of them, that the universe existed before their time. The world, as they imagine it, is young, simple, and artless as themselves. Jacqueline sees Miraut and Miraut sees Jacqueline right in the middle of it.

Miraut is far bigger and stronger than Jacqueline. When he puts his fore-paws on the child's shoulders, he towers a whole head and chest above her. He could eat her up in three mouthfuls; but he knows, he feels a virtue is in her, and that, small as she is, she is precious. He admires, he loves her. He licks her face out of pure affection. Jacqueline loves him because he is strong and kind. She has a great respect for him. She notices that he knows many secrets she does not, and that the mysterious genius of the earth is in him. She reveres him as men in olden days, under another sky, revered rustic, hairy gods of the woods and fields.

But one day she has a strange surprise that alarms, amazes her; she sees her venerated divinity, her genius of the earth, her hairy god, Miraut, tied by a long leash to a tree, beside the well. She gazes and wonders. Miraut looks at her out of his honest, patient eyes. Not knowing he is a divinity, a shaggy god, he wears his chain and collar without resentment. But Jacqueline hesitates, she dares not go nearer. She cannot understand her divine and mysterious friend being a prisoner, and a vague sadness fills her childish soul.

THE END